Murder by
Any Other Name

a collection of
509 Crime Stories

by Colin Conway

Murder by Any Other Name

Copyright © 2021 Colin Conway

Original Cover Design by Zach McCain
Updated Cover Design by Rob Williams

ISBN: 978-1-7371120-6-8

Original Ink Press, an imprint of High Speed Creative, LLC
1521 N. Argonne Road, #C-205
Spokane Valley, WA 99212

Visit the author's website at www.colinconway.com

Table of Contents

What is the 509?

Separated by the Cascade Range, Washington State is divided into two distinctly different climates and cultures.

The western side of the Cascades is home to Seattle, its 34 inches of annual rainfall, and the incredibly weird and smelly Gum Wall. Most of the state's wealth and political power are concentrated in and around this enormous city. The residents of this area know the prosperity that has come from being the home of Microsoft, Amazon, Boeing, and Starbucks.

To the east of the Cascade Mountains lies nearly two-thirds of the entire state, a lot of which is used for agriculture. Washington State leads the nation in producing apples, it is the second-largest potato grower, and it's the fourth for providing wheat.

This eastern part of the state can enjoy more than 170 days of sunshine each year, which is important when there are more than 200 lakes nearby. However, the beautiful summers are offset by harsh winters, with average snowfall reaching 47 inches and the average high hovering around 37°.

While five telephone area codes provide service to the westside, only 509 covers everything east of the Cascades, a staggering twenty-one counties.

Of these, Spokane County is the largest with an estimated population of 506,000.

Foreword

In William Shakespeare's *Romeo and Juliet*, one of the title characters asks, "What's in a name? That which we call a rose by any other name would smell as sweet." Over the years, this famous line has been paraphrased to, "A rose by any other name—" Well, you get the rest.

And with apologies to Bill, I like the latter version better. I'm a simple guy.

When creating this collection of short stories, I noticed an underlying theme—*murder*. Finding a thread like that might not make an ordinary person happy, but we writers are a weird bunch. We get excited by discoveries like that.

It's like learning that plants in your garden can be made into poison. *Oh, my God*, a scribbler of crime will think, *we can kill a character with oleander! And that killer could be a grandma*. Well, not my Nana, she's sweet. And not your grandma, either, because she's probably lovely like you. But someone else's grandma, for sure. Most likely that someone isn't reading my stories. I'll wager their grandma would have murderous tendencies.

Or maybe we writers notice a sad story about a man dying from a falling icicle. That's a senseless tragedy, for sure. Still, an author takes that idea, spins it into a revenge slaying with a sliver of ice, and when the cops arrive, the murder weapon has melted away along with any fingerprints.

I'm sure that same oleander-growing grandma was involved in that crime as well.

After noticing a thread of murder throughout this collection, I tried to determine if something linked them together. In other words, what was the motivation for such a heinous crime?

Were they of a passionate nature—the kind of killing a jilted lover might be involved in? Some of the stories were, but not all.

Were they of a calculated nature—the type of murders we usually expect in serial killer stories? Only one tale featured a homicide of this fashion.

Were they crimes of opportunity? A killing conducted as a means to another end. Yup, there were some of those.

So, ultimately, the murders were not connected by anything more than their proximity to the area code of 509. Sometimes that's how life is. We're connected to those around us by being in the right place at that right time.

Or, in the case of these murderous tales—the wrong place at the wrong time.

***

Which brings us to this book. These tales consist of hired killers, down on their luck criminals, and good people doing bad.

Some of the tales in this collection tie directly into the previous novels—*The Side Hustle*, *The Long Cold Winter*, *The Blind Trust*, *The Suit*, *The Value in Our Lies*, and *The Mean Street*.

There are tales in this collection that have no straight tie to the existing novels except that they occur in this area code. Some of these characters may end up in a future book or another short story. Many of the characters in *The Mean Street* first sprang to life in short stories. Sheriff Tom

Jessup originally appeared as a character in a quick tale, then later garnered a starring role in *The Blind Trust*.

And that goes to show that you never know who might pop up in the 509.

Colin Conway
Summer/2021

Murder by
Any Other Name

A Lonely Suffering

The sun shone through the living room window and woke Ronald Brenner from a dreamless sleep. As he sat upright on the couch, he grunted in response to the stiffness in his back and the deep pounding inside his head.

Brenner grabbed a soft pack of Marlboros from the coffee table. With a shake of his wrist, he loosened one, then lit it. The cigarette trembled in his hand while a wave of nausea traveled from his stomach up to his throat. He swallowed against the flow and was left with a burning in his esophagus.

Even though he'd only inhaled once on it, he crushed the Marlboro in the nearby ashtray.

Using the arm of the couch to steady himself, Brenner stood. He held onto the piece of furniture longer than was necessary, but he was afraid the room might suddenly spin.

It didn't.

He grunted again, then released the couch. He took a tentative step. Then another. Soon, he was walking.

Brenner passed through his bedroom on the way to the bathroom. On the bed, Donna Terrell lay in unbuttoned jeans and a light blue T-shirt shoved above her unclasped bra. He shook his head, immediately regretted the motion, and continued toward the shower.

***

An hour later, Brenner half-heartedly dipped a brush into a paint can. Yesterday he scraped a wire brush over the short picket fence that ran the perimeter of the property. Today was supposed to be the glory work. It didn't feel so glorious.

His head banged an out-of-rhythm cadence while he dragged the paintbrush up and down the various wood planks. The new white paint spitefully reflected the sun and caused his eyes to ache.

The door to his apartment opened, and Donna stepped tentatively out. She spotted him, then looked away with what Brenner would have described to a stranger as modesty, but he really knew to be shame. She glanced back at him, then hurried next door to her side of the duplex.

He sighed and studied the can of paint between his knees.

A cold beer from his refrigerator would have tasted nice right about then.

***

A couple of hours passed before Donna came back outside. By then, Brenner had made it to the other side of the yard. He dragged the brush with more pace and less care than before. His head hurt worse due to the squinting caused by the sun reflecting on the white paint.

He ruefully shook his head. He was a fool for thinking painting fence slats would be more enjoyable than scraping.

Donna waved at him—the cautious gesture of someone who didn't know the words necessary to start an awkward conversation. She sat on the front step of the porch that both units shared. Donna cupped her hands for a moment, then leaned her head back to exhale a thin line of smoke.

She didn't look in his direction again as she worked on her cigarette.

Brenner finished the plank he was painting, laid the brush across the top of the can, and stood. His knees popped, and there was a sharp pain in the middle of his shoulder blades. He rotated his neck and was rewarded with an additional pounding in his head. Slowly, Brenner ambled over to the porch and joined Donna.

He lit a cigarette for himself. "How you doing?"

She shrugged. Her long, dishwater blond hair was tucked behind her ears, but several strands hung loosely in front of her forehead.

"About last night—"

She waved a hand to stop him. "Don't do that."

"What?"

"Don't say you're sorry."

"That's not something I normally do."

Donna glanced at him before looking at her cigarette. "Me, neither."

They sat quietly for several minutes. Donna finally broke the silence. "I'm going to a meeting."

"They have one now?"

"It's not my usual."

She dropped her cigarette to the sidewalk and crushed it with the toe of her shoe. She reached into her pocket and pulled out a red plastic coin.

"Here," she said, handing it to Brenner. "That's my ninety-day chip."

He took the plastic coin, turning it over in his hand.

Donna pushed off the steps and stood. "The next time I come over asking for a drink—"

Brenner looked up expectantly.

"—tell me to fuck off."

She left then and didn't look back.

***

By the late afternoon, Brenner had finished painting, cleaned the brushes, and threw away the empty cans. He opened his first beer of the day as a reward for a job well done. He stood on the porch, sipping the cold drink, and appreciating how nice the white picket fence now looked.

In less than five minutes, he opened the second beer.

***

Brenner awoke on the couch to banging on Donna's door. The clock on the wall showed a few minutes after eight in the morning. He allowed himself a self-indulgent moan. There was no one around to tell him to keep it to himself, and the self-pity felt good. He moaned again.

The loud knocking next door continued.

He struggled upright and swallowed back the nausea he'd become accustomed to most mornings. Brenner tilted, swayed, and shuffled toward the front door.

Upon opening it, a tall police officer faced him.

"Go back inside, sir," was the quick, almost automatic response. The officer squinted for another beat before asking, "Ron?"

"Morning, Lee."

Officer Lee Sheets asked, "You live here?"

He nodded.

"Know how we can contact the landlord?"

"That's me." Brenner tapped his chest. "I own the place."

"Oh." Sheets looked toward Donna's door as if he expected it to open. It hadn't.

A noise at the front of the property caused Brenner to face another officer walking toward the duplex. This cop was several years younger than Sheets and carried a look of expectant confrontation.

Brenner asked Officer Sheets, "What's going on?"

"Does Donna Terrell live here?"

"Uh-huh."

"Got a key?"

The other officer stepped onto the porch. Brenner didn't like the way the younger man studied him. He eyed the older officer.

"Can you tell me what's going on?"

"Ms. Terrell was found this morning in Riverfront Park."

Brenner closed his eyes and took a deep breath. After a moment, he slowly released it and opened his eyes. Both officers now watched him.

"How did it happen?" Brenner asked.

"Homicide."

"Meaning what?"

"There's no medical opinion, yet," Sheets said.

Brenner sighed. "Give it your best guess, Lee."

"Strangled."

"Damn it," Brenner whispered.

"Can you let us into her apartment?" the young officer asked.

"Without a warrant?"

The two officers stared at him.

Brenner shrugged and stepped back into his apartment.

***

While the officers secured Donna's apartment, Brenner sat on his couch and lit a cigarette. The familiar pounding in his head played out a new rhythm, and he fought for control of his stomach.

He and Donna had had sex the night before while they drank. It was fast and clumsy, and when they finished, they morosely poured themselves another shot to toast their carnal knowledge of the other.

Brenner shouldn't have done it. First, she was his tenant, which meant she paid him rent—money he sorely needed. Second, she was becoming his friend. That, in itself, was bad business. Sleeping with her was plain stupid.

Now she was dead and may still have some of his DNA on her body. He didn't know if his DNA would remain that long. He considered telling the officers now on the porch but thought better of it. He was not well-liked in the department anymore. Time wouldn't heal those wounds.

When they finished locking the apartment, the officers secured a line of yellow POLICE—DO NOT ENTER—tape over the door.

Lee Sheets stepped into Brenner's apartment. "Ron, do you have any next of kin info?"

Brenner shook his head.

"Did you know her well?"

"She lived here for about six months. We talked now and then."

"She ever worry about anyone?"

"No. She never said anything like that."

"Huh." Sheets glanced around the apartment. "Haven't seen you around in some time. How've you been?"

Suddenly embarrassed about the lack of cleanliness in his home, Brenner mumbled, "Doing good."

The officer looked around once more, then said, "Well, you take care, Ron."

"You, too."

When the door clicked behind Officer Sheets, Brenner walked purposefully into the kitchen and grabbed a bottle of Jim Beam.

It was 10:17 a.m.

***

Shortly after nine in the evening, Brenner bolted upright from his bed and ran into the bathroom. The toilet seat banged against the tank, and he dropped to his knees. He grasped the bowl and retched—repeatedly.

Tears filled his eyes, and he wanted to die.

After everything was out of his stomach and the dry heaves began, he even asked for God to kill him.

God didn't listen.

Brenner rolled onto his butt and leaned against the bathtub. He hung his head and fell asleep for some time.

When he awoke again, he went into the kitchen. He had no idea how long he'd been asleep or how long he'd thrown up, but it was now after midnight. He sat at the table and held his head in his hands.

Donna was dead, and he might end up being a suspect. If his DNA somehow were matched, the detectives investigating the case wouldn't be sympathetic to his position. He'd burned those bridges years ago.

The longer he sat there, the more an idea began to germinate. Maybe there was something he could do to help his situation. He rolled around the concept for a bit.

When he accepted that he could help himself, he returned to bed and slept through the night.

***

In the morning, Brenner went to the downtown library and asked a short, gray-haired woman at the counter to help him look up the Alcoholics Anonymous meeting schedule in Spokane.

"You don't know how to use a computer?"

"I don't have one," Brenner said.

"You can use ours." She pointed to four rows of computers. "Anyone can use them."

"I'm not interested."

"Not interested? Are you a Luddite?"

"I'm retired."

The desk clerk frowned, shook her head, but still turned to her computer. "Alcoholics Anonymous," she muttered as her fingers clicked about the keyboard. "Here it is." She printed off a page filled with meeting times and places.

Brenner thanked her, then took the list to a table and sat alone. He pulled Donna's red chip from his pocket and studied it. On the front was a triangle with the words *Unity*, *Service*, and *Recovery* along its sides. Inside the shape were the words *3-Month*.

The prayer about God granting serenity, courage, and wisdom was on the opposite side of the chip. He set the plastic trinket down and turned his attention to the list.

Meetings were held throughout the county, and they were listed by days of the week. There was a separate list for those meetings held daily. Brenner didn't think Donna went every day. He wasn't sure when her regular sessions were, but that didn't matter. He knew she left him Sunday just before two.

There was only one meeting on that day around that time—Come All Ye Faithful in Recovery—and they met at the First Baptist Church. It was a women's group, and it didn't meet again until next Sunday.

***

"I'd like to speak with someone about the women's AA meeting that meets on Sunday."

With his hands clasped together and hanging in front of his waist, Doug Wallace, the pastor of the First Baptist Church, said, "If you're looking for help—"

Brenner lifted a hand to interrupt the man. "That's not the kind of help I need."

They were in Wallace's office—a small, modest place with books stacked everywhere. Photographs of various faces lined the walls.

Brenner continued. "My friend was murdered after she attended the meeting held here. At least, I think she attended the meeting. All I want to do is ask someone a couple questions. That's it."

"Recovery is a private affair. Who you're looking for may not want their affliction known."

Brenner pointed to the phone. "Call them and ask. Can you do that? I'll be on the front steps. If they'll talk with me, I'll wait until they can get here. If they don't want to talk, then I'll come back Sunday for the meeting."

"It's supposed to be a private meeting. For those seeking help."

"Murder isn't private," Brenner said. "Either they talk to me today, or I'll come back on Sunday. I'm trying to be accommodating. Please let them know that."

Pastor Wallace nodded. "Wait outside, and I'll make the call."

***

Eighty-seven minutes later, Brenner considered giving up. An hour and a half was more than enough time to get from anywhere in the county to this church.

While he waited patiently, sitting on the steps of the church, his stomach started to ache, and he began to sweat. This soon turned into full cramps that lasted some time. When they passed, he breathed a sigh of relief. They'd be back, he knew—the stomach cramps always returned.

Now, he wanted a beer in the worst way. He could almost taste it. After the cramps passed, he promised himself to stop at the Lamplighter on the way home and get a quick one. That seemed to make him feel better.

Across the street, a heavyset woman paused and looked in both directions before crossing. She approached the church directly until she stopped in front of Brenner. She crossed her arms and clenched her jaw. Suspicion filled her eyes.

He stood. "Are you from the AA group?"

The woman nodded once.

"I'm Ron," he said and extended his hand.

She kept her arms folded and continued to stare at him.

He shrugged and shoved both hands into his pockets. "My friend was murdered yesterday."

"I'm sorry."

"When she left her house, I think she came here."

"You were with her when she left?"

"We talked." The image of Donna asking him to tell her to go away the next time she wanted a drink flashed through his mind. "She said she was going to a meeting."

The woman shifted her weight onto a single leg. "I don't know what you've heard, but we don't talk about those who attend our meetings. That's why it's called anonymous."

Brenner cocked his head. "She's dead. You don't need to protect her identity."

"Are you a cop?"

"I was."

"Was? Why aren't the real cops talking with me?"

"They don't know she came here. If you want me to tell them, I will. They'll have a uniform stop by your work to conduct an interview. Maybe they'll even come by the meeting on Sunday, remake the acquaintance of some of your members."

The woman frowned. "You're an unpleasant man. Do you know that?"

With his hands still in his pockets, Brenner leaned forward. "Someone murdering my friend tends to make me angry."

The woman squeezed her arms tighter around her body. "Who was she?"

"Donna Terrell."

"We don't have any regulars named Donna, and we don't use last names."

"It wasn't her usual meeting."

The woman stared at Brenner.

"She went because she—" He couldn't say the word.

The woman said it for him. "Slipped. She drank when she wasn't supposed to."

Brenner nodded.

"Were you with her when it happened?"

"She lives in my duplex, and she's my friend."

"That avoided my question."

Brenner was uncomfortable with the honesty, but he answered, nonetheless. "We drank together, yes."

The woman looked up and down the street before returning her gaze to Ronald. "She was here on Sunday. I talked with her."

"Did she leave with anyone from the group?"

"I don't think so. No."

"Did she say if she was meeting anyone afterward?"

The woman unfolded her arms. "She said she was going to meet her sponsor."

"Do you know who that is?"

"No."

"How would I track that person down?"

"She said her regular meetings were at St. Michael's. Go there. Ask for her sponsor. That's the best I can tell you. I've gotta go."

After the woman left, Brenner sat again on the church's stairs and pulled out the AA schedule.

The Early Bird Gets the Recovery meetings were at St. Michael's Catholic Church on East Sprague, Monday through Friday, at six in the morning.

Jesus and recovery started early, Brenner thought.

Now that he knew he couldn't do anything more, he stood and put the folded AA schedule back into his pocket.

He headed toward the Lamplighter. He had the rest of the day to deal with his guilt.

***

The alarm went off at five, and Brenner angrily turned it off. With his head hurting and stomach aching, he struggled to sit up. He'd even gone to bed early, but with a stomach full of Jim Beam and beer, a decent sleep had been elusive.

He showered and shaved, hoping to look like his former self. He dropped Visine into his eyes, but the cooling sensation did little for the redness. He wore jeans, a white-collared shirt, and a brown sport coat.

A few minutes before six, the backroom of St. Michael's church already teemed with activity. Roughly twenty people stood around and chatted softly. A thin woman in faded green cargo pants and a cream-colored T-shirt walked up. She held out her hand and said, "I'm Joan."

He gently took her hand. "Ron."

Joan's smile was closed-lipped. "Welcome, Ron. Ever been to a meeting before?"

"I'm not here for the meeting."

"You're not?"

"I'm looking for Donna's sponsor."

Her face darkened, and she stepped back.

"I'm Donna's friend." When the woman didn't say anything, Brenner continued. "Were you aware she was murdered?"

Joan's eyes widened, and she covered her mouth with a hand. She glanced over at a gray-haired man holding a Styrofoam cup. "Hardy," she muttered. "Hardy was her sponsor."

Brenner nodded his thanks, then headed toward the man.

When the sponsor saw him approaching, he kindly smiled and said, "Good morning."

"You were Donna's sponsor?"

His smile faded. "Excuse me?"

"You met with her on Sunday afternoon."

Hardy glanced around before refocusing on Brenner. "I can't discuss that with you."

Brenner opened his mouth to protest, but Hardy interrupted him.

"Listen. She'll be here soon enough. If you want to ask her something, you can do it then. If she talks with you, so be it. But if she wants you out of this meeting, I'll toss you out myself."

"Donna's dead."

Hardy's mouth opened in surprise.

"Murdered," Brenner continued. "Sunday evening some time. Maybe even Monday morning."

Hardy blinked several times before asking, "Are you a cop?"

Realizing a lie would make it easier to get the info he wanted, Brenner said, "Yes."

Hardy sat on a folding chair, his eyes never leaving Brenner's.

"You met with her Sunday afternoon?"

Hardy nodded.

"What was discussed?"

"She slipped and drank. That scared her."

The image of Donna lying on his bed with her pants unbuttoned and her shirt shoved up over her breasts flashed in Brenner's mind. He jerked his head in hopes of shaking it free.

Hardy stared into his cup. "I reminded her that sobriety was a lifelong journey and mistakes happen. It's not the end of the world."

"Did she say anything else?"

"She said—" Hardy's face flushed, and his voice softened. "She said she'd gone to bed with her neighbor."

Brenner's heart raced. If the cops ever found Hardy, he would share that info with them. Of course, it wouldn't mean Brenner killed Donna, but it could mean they would look at him as a suspect. Brenner focused his attention back on Hardy.

"Did you get his name?"

"The neighbor?" Hardy looked away. "No."

"Does it embarrass you to talk about her indiscretion?"

Hardy frowned now. "It's not that. It's just that she shouldn't get involved with anyone while in the program. She didn't need the extra pressure a relationship would bring."

"You blushed, though."

"I did? I wasn't aware of that. I guess I'm not used to sharing someone else's secrets."

"Where did you meet to talk?"

"The Hoot Owl." Hardy pointed in the general direction of the café. "It's our normal after-meeting place. Most of the group go there throughout the week."

"What time did you meet?"

"Around two."

"Where did she go after you talked?"

Hardy shrugged. "How would I know? She said she had some thinking to do and left."

"Thinking?"

"That's what she said."

"How long were you her sponsor?"

"About three months."

"Did she ever mention problems with anyone?"

"No."

"Ever mention a boyfriend?"

"No."

The attendees moved toward their seats. Hardy glanced around and stood. "The meeting's about to start. I'm leading today." He shuffled to the front.

Brenner sat on one of the folding metal chairs in the rear of the room. The meeting began, and soon the attendees were invited to speak. Ronald sat through several admissions, each one making him despise the confessor for their weakness.

When he couldn't take it anymore, he left. He walked to his car, climbed in, and turned on the radio. He listened to the news for a while, not really paying attention and not really caring.

He now knew where Donna went after leaving him but was no closer to finding out who killed her.

***

The following day, Brenner awoke with a start and bolted for the bathroom. He vomited before he could lift the toilet seat. Puke covered his arm, the back of the toilet lid, and the seat. Seeing and smelling the sick everywhere, Brenner retched again.

He didn't stop until his insides were empty, and he lay on the bathroom floor with his face pressed against the cold porcelain of the toilet.

While his head throbbed, Brenner allowed himself to groan. He didn't know why, but the self-pitying moans always seemed to make him feel a little better.

After he cleaned himself up, he sat in his underwear on the couch and grabbed a pack of cigarettes. Before lighting one, he saw Donna's three-month chip and picked it up.

He studied the plastic coin for several minutes before making his decision.

***

Brenner made the meeting a few minutes late. Joan greeted him at the door. "More questions?" she whispered.

"Not this time."

Joan waved toward the rows of folding metal chairs. "Grab a seat. I'll check on you afterward."

***

"It's depressing," Brenner said.

Joan ran her finger around the edge of her coffee mug. "It can be, but I look at it this way. There is hope in those stories. When we admit our failings, when we accept we're human and make mistakes, we change course. We start to heal and help those around us. That's a pretty exciting thing."

Brenner considered his half-empty coffee mug. "How long have you been in the program?"

"Four years."

He sipped his coffee then and looked around the Hoot Owl. Several others from the earlier meeting were there, sitting in groups and murmuring. A waitress moved from table to table, refilling coffee cups and bantering with her customers.

"Are you coming back?" Joan asked.

Brenner shrugged.

"What's stopping you?"

Another shrug.

Her smile was soft and full of understanding. "You'll know when it's the right time."

Brenner stared into the black liquid held by his cup. "Would you like to have dinner with me?"

"It depends."

He looked up. "On what?"

"Two things. If you're going to another meeting, and if you'll find a sponsor."

"Will you be my sponsor?"

Joan's face flattened. "No."

"Why not?"

"Getting involved with your sponsor is a bad idea. It's not healthy. The sponsor is supposed to be there for support. You can't mix relationship issues into that and expect everything to work correctly."

Brenner nodded and stared at his coffee again.

"I think that's why Donna was having so much trouble at the end and why she slipped."

"What do you mean?"

"She got involved with Hardy."

"You mean—"

Joan nodded. "Too many emotions get wrapped up in a relationship like that."

***

Brenner knocked on the door for apartment #2.

It had taken some asking around at the Hoot Owl, but someone finally knew where Hardy lived. At first, Joan was reluctant to help him. When Brenner explained what he believed, she helped him get the information. She refused to confront Hardy—she wanted Brenner to call the cops. He said he would after he confirmed what he believed.

Brenner knocked harder on the door, and Hardy slowly opened it. His hair was a mess, and his eyelids drooped. His words slurred as he spoke. "Whaddaya want?"

"You were involved with Donna."

Hardy tried to close the door. Brenner caught it with his hand and pushed it fully open. Hardy stumbled backward, tripped over his own feet, and fell to the floor.

Brenner stepped in and swung the door shut behind him. The apartment was a mess, and a stack of beer cans was on the coffee table.

"You're drunk."

"So?"

"You found out about Donna."

Hardy tried to get up, but Brenner shoved him back to the floor.

"You loved her, didn't you?"

With almost closed eyes, Hardy sneered. "Slut."

Brenner slapped the man across the face. Hardy jerked, and his eyes widened. Brenner slapped him on the opposite cheek—this time with the back of his hand.

"Hey!" Hardy yelled. "You can't do that!"

"Me." Brenner tapped his chest. "She was with me."

Hardy tilted his head to the side. "Huh?"

"I was the one she was with before—"

The man's eyes widened with realization. "You!" Hardy struggled to get up, but Brenner pushed him back to the floor.

"We were friends, and she never mentioned your name."

Hardy frantically tried to stand, but Brenner hopped and jumped wherever the man moved, then shoved him back to the floor.

"That bitch!" Hardy yelled, and Brenner slapped him again.

Hardy screamed and lunged at Brenner's legs. He managed to wrap his arms around them and awkwardly drag Brenner to the ground.

"That bitch!" Hardy scampered atop Brenner. He wildly swung his fists while he continued to yell insults at Donna.

Brenner moved his head as he tried to avoid the blows raining down. He pushed and squirmed under Hardy's weight, but it had been years since he'd practiced any wrestling or ground fighting.

"Bitch!" Hardy landed a punch on the side of Brenner's cheek. "Got what she deserved."

Brenner grabbed Hardy's shirt with his left hand. He pulled downward at the same time he punched upward. He had planned to hit Hardy in the face, but when he yanked on the man, it jerked him forward instead of down. Brenner's punch caught the other man directly in the throat.

Hardy jerked upright and clasped his hands over his neck. He opened his mouth to suck for air and wheezed helplessly.

Brenner shoved him aside. With a quick twist of his body, he was free. He stood over Hardy.

When the man finally could breathe, he began to cry. "I didn't mean it," he rasped.

Brenner didn't know if Hardy meant he didn't intend to kill Donna, or he didn't mean to call her a bitch repeatedly, but he wasn't going to ask any more questions to find out.

He kicked Hardy in the head.

***

Former Senior Patrol Officer Ronald Brenner walked into the Public Safety Building. After he cleared the security checkpoint, he announced himself at the front desk. He waited for several minutes for a detective to appear through the double doors to the hallway of the Spokane Police Department. Detective Glenn Higgins walked toward Ronald.

"Been a long time," Higgins said. "I didn't think you'd show your face around here again."

Brenner shoved his hands in his pockets. "A friend was murdered. I know who killed her."

Higgins closely watched Brenner.

"I'll tell you what I know, and then I'll leave."

The detective turned and walked to the double doors. He opened one and motioned for Brenner. "Let's go," he said with an irritated wave of his hand.

Brenner followed the detective through the hallways as years of memories flooded back to him. Several eyes turned his way—some even belonged to former friends. He didn't bother smiling, nodding, or even saying hello. Those opportunities were long gone.

Instead, he quietly trailed behind Detective Higgins until they arrived at an interview room. It couldn't have been more than eight feet by eight feet.

"I'll grab a notepad," the detective said. "Wait here."

The fluorescent lights overhead flickered and hummed loudly. The room smelled of body odor. Brenner believed the walls were moving ever so slightly inward as he took a seat at the small table.

Above him, there was a small bulb that was dark. When it illuminated red, it meant he was being recorded, both audio and video. He stared at it for some time, expecting it to light up. It never did. Eventually, he pulled his gaze from it.

His hands felt clammy, and he rubbed them together. That didn't help get rid of the moisture, so he brushed them along his pants.

The walls moved again. He was sure of it. The room had already gotten slightly smaller. Brenner knew this was a trick of his mind—that he just had to hold it together for a bit longer. Once he told Detective Higgins his story, he could get the hell out of there.

How long did it take for a guy to retrieve a notepad?

A couple of years ago, Ronald Brenner promised himself he would never return to this building. He also promised himself that he would never again get put into one of these small rooms.

But here he was.

He wanted a drink. He removed Donna's three-month chip from his pocket to read the Serenity Prayer. He rubbed the edge of the plastic coin and began to recite the words.

Almost as soon as he started, he stopped. The words sounded so stupid. He didn't want serenity, courage, or wisdom.

He wanted a bottle of Jim Beam.

Ronald Brenner angrily shoved the plastic coin back into his pocket.

He'd stop at the store on the way home—maybe he'd get two bottles.

The Death of Wilbur Pennington

It was the music I noticed first.

The sound—Mozart's serenade known as "Eine Kleine Nachtmusik"—came softly from a speaker in the corner of the room.

In the opposite corner sat a red wingback chair with an opened book face down on its arm.

A black and red Oriental rug covered most of the hardwood floor.

Thick burgundy curtains covered the windows that lined the south wall of the room. The curtains muffled the noise from the street.

Custom-made bookshelves—filled from top to bottom—lined the entirety of the north wall. A rolling ladder stood stoically in front of the shelves, waiting to be pushed or pulled to retrieve some rarely used tome from a perch high above.

Silence briefly replaced the music. I started to move but paused as a new haunting sound entered the room. I closed my eyes for a moment to enjoy Pachelbel's "Canon."

"The hell are you grinning at?"

"Pachelbel," I said.

"Pennington."

I opened my eyes and stared at the short man standing next to me. His lips twisted in a mocking smirk, and his eyebrows had climbed up his forehead.

"Wilbur Pennington," he said and pointed. "Remember him? The dead guy?"

I looked back into the room at the body in the middle of the beautiful Oriental rug.

He lay on his back with his eyes wide open. He appeared to be in his early sixties. His hair was silver with dark flecks. He wore a tan Polo shirt, black slacks, and black loafers.

I stood outside the room in the foyer. I still hadn't entered the potential crime scene. The cause of death wasn't apparent. The man could simply have had a heart attack and died in his reading room. Maybe there was something more, but on the surface, everything seemed boringly normal.

Two uniformed deputies watched me closely. One looked slightly familiar. The other was a rookie or near enough since I'd never seen him before.

Sergeant Anderson waited impatiently next to me, his hands firmly on his ample hips. His bitter smirk had remained in place since reminding me of the deceased. Anderson was a short, arrogant man that I disliked for many years and for reasons beyond his stature and disposition. He cocked his head as if expecting me to say something.

"How was he found?" I asked.

"A nine-one-one hang up." Anderson jerked his head toward the deputies. "Morton and Posluszny were dispatched. They came out and found him. No signs of struggle. He probably had a heart attack and died. He lives alone. No pets. We checked the bedrooms, two of them, in case you're wondering, and didn't find anything that might belong to someone else."

My cell phone vibrated, and I pulled it from my pocket to find a text message from Laura.

DINNER TONIGHT?

My fingers tapped the keypad. Sounds good. Miss
You.

I tucked the phone away and pointed at the deputy, who
seemed familiar. "You're Morton?"

He nodded.

"When you got here, what did you see?"

"The front door was open, but the screen was closed—
no sign of forced entry. We could see the body from there
and immediately entered. The first thing I did was check
for vitals. We called it in, and Fire responded. They
pronounced him dead and left."

"Did they touch anything?"

"Besides Pennington? No."

"Can we speed this up, Chambers?" The sergeant had
crossed his arms over his chest. "We've got calls stacking
up out there, and I don't want my guys standing around
dicking the dog while you work this out in your slow-ass
way."

"Dicking the dog?"

"You know what I mean."

I turned back to Morton. "I didn't notice a phone in the
library. Are there any in the house?"

"There's one in the bedroom and a cordless in the
kitchen."

I pointed to the other deputy, who had the wide-eyed
gaze that all rookies wear. "What's your name?"

"Earl, sir. Earl Posluszny."

I thumbed toward Morton. "Is he your training officer?"

"Final rotation, sir."

"Well, impress me so he can write something nice about
you in a report."

Posluszny glanced at his training deputy before
speaking. "Well, sir, someone called nine-one-one, and

there wasn't a phone near the victim. Also, we didn't find a cell phone. If he had a heart attack, the phone would be near where he fell. I mean, that's the way I figured it. So, someone else called for emergency services."

Morton smiled, proud of his recruit.

Pachelbel's piece ended, and a new one started. It was something I had never heard before, but it was beautiful, nonetheless.

"Sergeant," I said, "we need a forensic team."

***

Anderson left before the lab technicians arrived. When they did, I sent Morton and Posluszny out to canvass the neighborhood for potential witnesses. That meant a lot of door-knocking and smiling at citizens—a perfect task for a training officer and his recruit.

I wandered the exterior of the house and didn't notice anything out of place or suspicious.

Then I searched the remainder of the home, looking for something that might seem useful. In Pennington's bedroom, I found a copy of *Lolita* on his nightstand. It's considered a classic, but I found it boring and rambling when I read it years ago. I quit halfway into Vladimir Nabokov's pedophiliac tale of Humbert Humbert's obsession. I opened this copy of the book and discovered it was written in Spanish.

That gave me pause.

Would I have found the book more interesting if I read it in another language? I don't speak Spanish and have a rudimentary knowledge of French—high school level. I doubt another language would have changed my opinion of that book.

After another glance at the cover, I put the book back where I found it.

Not having found anything of evidentiary value, I ended my search and returned to the living room. The music was still playing as the technicians finished their work. It was Wagner's "The Ride of the Valkyries." It was a surreal, almost delightful moment as the technicians completed their duties to a soundtrack. I've experienced a lot of things in my career, but this was a first.

Suddenly, I stiffened.

The music.

I didn't know where it originated. There was a speaker in the room but no stereo system. As I moved throughout the house, it dawned on me the music was everywhere.

It took some searching, but I finally located the stereo in a kitchen pantry. When I flung open the doors, the music reached a crescendo. Unfortunately, I was disappointed I hadn't found an important clue. Wagner's magnificent song seemed to be fitting for that type of moment. I left the music playing and returned to the technicians.

"What did you find?" I asked.

The lead technician, a nice-looking woman with red hair and a face full of freckles, walked over. "No trauma to the body. Nothing under his fingernails. Nothing out of the ordinary."

"Did you pull prints off the telephones?"

"Of course. We got prints off the one in the bedroom. The cordless in the kitchen was wiped clean."

My brow furrowed. "No prints?"

"That's usually what 'wiped clean' means."

"Interesting."

She patted my shoulder. "That's why you're the detective, Chambers." She and the other technicians gathered their equipment and left.

After thirty minutes, the coroner's team showed up to take Pennington. When they were gone, I was alone in the house. This was an unusual situation and one most officers tried to avoid. Having others around protects people from corrupt cops stealing and keeps good cops from getting accused of the same. I used my radio to call Morton to come back to the house and secure it. He and his rookie could string the DO NOT CROSS tape and make it a training exercise.

While I waited, I sat in the red wingback chair and picked up the book he must have been reading. It was a hardback version of Mickey Spillane's *I, The Jury*. I checked the copyright—a first edition printed in 1947. I read the two pages he was on but didn't learn anything of value, except Spillane wasn't my thing.

For a moment, I pondered the difference in styles of Spillane's and Nabokov's books. One was a ham-fisted mystery, and the other was overly praised drivel. Then there was the apparent difference in language—one was in English, the other Spanish. Perhaps the man was reading two books at once. I did that often, sometimes juggling three books—one at my bedside, another at my desk, and the final one in my car for those moments when I had time to kill.

I climbed the ladder and looked at the books on the upper shelves. Nothing appeared out of place or suggested it might be a clue to what happened to Pennington. I hadn't expected to find anything up there. I'd simply never climbed a bookshelf ladder before and wanted to do it.

After a time, I moved to the front porch. Being alone in the house bothered me. Not because of the recent death, but due to the appearance of impropriety.

While I continued to wait for the training officer and his rookie, a mail carrier walked up.

"How you doin'?" he said and passed by to drop several letters in the mailbox.

"Fine," I muttered as he walked away. "Just fine."

I removed the letters from the mailbox. Three envelopes were inside: a bill from the power company, a credit card application from Mastercard, and one with a return address of Spotless Cleaning Service.

Knowing I shouldn't open it without a warrant, I held the last envelope up to the sun. It took some time, but I made out what appeared to be an invoice.

Wilbur Pennington had a housekeeper.

***

The office for Spotless Cleaning Service was near the intersection of Mallon Avenue and Monroe Street. It was within shouting distance of the Public Safety Building, the home of both the Spokane County Sheriff's Office and the Spokane Police Department.

The janitorial company's home was clean and freshly painted, which one would expect. Once inside the office, it smelled of disinfectant, and everything appeared recently wiped down. Nonetheless, dust particles floated in the sunlight beaming through windows. The woman behind the receptionist's desk was in her mid-fifties. The name plaque on her desk read *Hazel Stilson*. She smiled broadly right before she asked if I needed help.

Her smile faded when I revealed my badge.

I showed her a page from my notebook. "Was anyone from your company at this address today?"

"Did something happen?"

"I need confirmation on the address."

Hazel opened a scheduling program on her computer. "Juanita Flores was scheduled to clean that house today."

"What's her address and phone number?"

It took a moment, but the receptionist printed Juanita's employment information and handed it to me.

"Is there something we should be worried about with her?"

"Not at this point."

Hazel frowned. Her opinion of Juanita Flores changed when I asked for her info, and I doubt anything would change it back.

***

Juanita lived on Dean Street in the West Central neighborhood, only about six blocks from the Spotless Cleaning Service building.

Nicknamed "The Zone," West Central had fallen on hard times over the past fifty years. As the affluent moved to the fringes of the city, West Central ended up with the poor.

I knocked on the front door of Juanita's house and soon heard movement inside. A moment later, the front door opened, and a boy, roughly ten years old, stood in front of me.

"Is your mother home?" I asked.

He stared at the gun on my hip and yelled, "Mama!"

A Hispanic woman came to the door.

"Juanita Flores?" I asked.

She nodded.

"I'm Detective Tim Chambers. Spokane County Sheriff's Office."

Juanita looked at the boy, who spoke rapidly in Spanish. Juanita's eyes returned to me and widened.

I stepped into the house and shut the door. "What's your name?" I asked the boy.

"Alex." His eyes carefully examined the badge on my belt.

"Alex, will you translate for me?"

His eyes brightened, and he smiled broadly.

"Ask your mother if she knows a man named Wilbur Pennington."

Alex translated, and Juanita nodded.

"Did she clean his house today?"

Again, Alex rattled off some Spanish.

Juanita said, "*Si*," and looked at me with confusion.

I didn't wait for Alex's translation. "Is she reading *Lolita*?"

"What's *Lolita*?" the boy asked.

"A book."

Juanita watched Alex as he spoke. She looked at me and shook her head.

"Alex," I said, waiting for him to look my way, "is your mother dating Wilbur Pennington?"

Alex shrugged before speaking. Juanita stared at me like I had lost my mind.

For a moment, I wondered if I should call for a translator.

"Ask her if she knows what happened to Wilbur today."

Alex and his mother spoke for a minute before he turned back to me. "Mr. Pennington was gone when she cleaned his house this morning."

The *Lolita* book on his nightstand was in Spanish. Juanita denied the book was hers. Maybe it really was Pennington's. However, when I flipped through some of his other books, all of them were in English.

"Did Wilbur speak Spanish?" I asked.

Alex spoke quickly, and Juanita held up her hand—her thumb and forefinger were less than an inch apart. If he could barely speak Spanish, he wouldn't read *Lolita*.

"Does your mother know if Wilbur was dating someone who spoke Spanish?"

Alex translated the question for his mother, who nodded and answered. When she finished, the boy said, "The lady works with him. My mother doesn't know her name, but she's seen her with Mr. Pennington. He called her his *gatita*."

"*Gatita*?"

Alex smiled. "Kitten. He called her his kitten."

"Where does Wilbur work?"

Alex spoke with his mother. They had several back and forths before he turned to me. "The college."

"Which college?"

Alex shrugged. "I asked her that. She does not know. She only knows at the college."

I paused with my questions to write in my notebook, and Juanita said something to Alex. When she finished speaking, the boy looked up and waited until I stopped writing. "What happened to Mr. Pennington?"

I thought about a gentle way to break the news but finally said, "He died."

Alex translated it back to his mother. Juanita looked sad, but not like a heartbroken lover might. Juanita spoke to Alex again.

The boy said, "She thought he was a nice man."

***

I radioed dispatch and asked for a translator to meet us at the station. A somewhat irritated man informed me the quickest a translator could be there was in ninety minutes.

Juanita and Alex sat quietly in the backseat of my unmarked car. The boy's eyes locked onto the Mobile Data Computer during the entire trip to the station.

I escorted them to an interview room and asked them to wait for the interpreter.

"You're not in trouble," I said to Juanita. Then I asked Alex to translate that for his mother.

Her eyes remained wide, but she nodded in understanding.

"Would you like anything to drink? Water or a soda?"

"A Coke," Alex said with a bright smile. Then he turned to his mother, and they had a rapid-fire exchange. When he faced me again, he said, "She won't have anything. Me neither."

"You're sure?"

"Yeah," he said, disappointed.

I left them alone after that.

At my desk, I started my computer and called up Google. I typed "Wilbur Pennington Spokane" into the search box and was promptly rewarded with one hundred thirteen hits.

The most common result showed the man to be an English professor at Eastern Washington University. I bounced around the college's website for a bit, looking for more information on him. The only thing I found was basic marketing fluff.

***

After completing an official interview with Juanita, a uniformed deputy drove her and her son home. The interview didn't provide any new information, but it would now be usable in court if ever needed.

It was almost four o'clock when I contacted the university. I spoke to the Dean of the English Department and explained what had occurred. She informed me that Pennington didn't have any classes scheduled that day but did have two the next.

I asked if she had time to meet tomorrow, and she agreed.

"I'll be out in the morning," I said and ended the call.

***

That night, Laura and I met for dinner at Anthony's. I requested a table on the deck overlooking the river. The sun was setting, and the night sky was bright orange.

Laura's golden walnut hair was pulled back with a clip. She wore a yellow sundress with sandals. It was summer beauty, and she wore it well.

She grabbed my hand across the table. "I'm glad to see you tonight."

"How did you get out on a Wednesday night?"

"He's watching a game with his friends at some bar in the Valley. So, I told him I was going to meet my sister."

"What happens if he calls her?"

Laura smiled and put her other hand on mine. "She knows about us. She's wanted me to leave Richard for years."

"So have I."

Her smile vanished. "Stop it."

***

She slipped out of bed around ten-thirty. I knew she was leaving, but I pretended to be asleep. Once she was gone, I got up, walked to the kitchen, and sat. It had been almost two years since I started seeing her. My marriage ended just before we met. She seemed a lifeline back to happiness.

I wanted Laura to leave Richard. She said she would, but it never happened. It was always one reason or another. Maybe her marriage wasn't perfect, but in some weird way, it worked for her.

I didn't know how much longer this situation would work for me.

***

The following morning, I headed straight to Cheney, the home of Eastern Washington University. I had graduated from there almost twenty-five years ago.

The dean was in Showalter Hall, which acts as the administrative building and is at the campus's heart. She was an attractive woman in her early fifties. Her light brown hair was highlighted and tucked behind her ears. She held out her hand, and her grip was confident.

"Dean Rawlings," she said as a way of introduction.

Her first name was Susan. I'd learned that from the college's website, but this was official business. A first name wasn't necessary.

"Detective Chambers," I said, introducing myself.

Her office was large with a dark wood desk and matching cabinets. Binders filled the cabinets. Framed degrees hung on the wall interspersed with photographs of Susan climbing various mountains.

She said, "After our conversation yesterday, I asked around. It appears there was a romance going on between Wilbur and Elisa Rodriguez. Please understand the university frowns upon our staff having interoffice relationships."

"I understand," I said and wrote the woman's name in my notebook.

"It seems most of our staff were aware of this situation, even though Wilbur and Elisa attempted to hide it."

I made another note while the dean continued. "To make matters worse, Elisa is a married woman."

For a brief moment, I thought of Laura. "Where can I find her?"

Susan checked a schedule on her desk. "She should be finishing a class in about ten minutes. Her next isn't until the afternoon. I'll walk you to her office."

"What does Elisa teach?"

"Spanish and English as a Second Language."

"Did you tell her about Wilbur's death?"

"I haven't told anyone," she said. "I thought I'd leave that to you."

***

As we entered her office, Elisa Rodriguez stood and greeted Dean Rawlings with a smile.

She was a short, dark-skinned woman who wore her hair in a tight bun. Elisa appeared to be in her late forties. She wore tortoiseshell-framed reading glasses.

"Elisa," Susan said, "this is Detective Chambers."

"Detective?"

"Yes, ma'am," I said. "Spokane County Sheriff's Office."

Elisa's brow furrowed. "What's going on?"

"I need to ask you some questions about Wilbur Pennington."

The professor looked at Susan and then back at me. "What's this about?"

"Is it true you were having an affair with Mr. Pennington?" I asked.

Elisa glanced at Susan. This time, she didn't say anything.

"Dean Rawlings," I said, "would you give us a few minutes?"

Susan nodded and left without a word.

The professor sat, removed her reading glasses, and crossed her arms over her chest. "Why does it matter what I do in my personal life? It's not a crime."

I sat in the chair on the other side of her desk. "It's not a crime," I assured her. "However, Wilbur died yesterday."

Susan's eyes widened.

"I don't think it was an accident."

Tears filled her eyes. "Oh, God."

It took several minutes for Elisa to compose herself. When she was able to answer some questions, I asked her for the correct spelling of her name and her address and added that information to my notebook.

"How long have you and Wilbur been seeing each other?"

"Five months," she said and dabbed at her eyes with a tissue.

Her accent was notable, but her English was perfect.

"When was the last time you saw Wilbur?"

"A couple of nights ago. We had dinner at his house."

"A couple meaning two?"

"That's correct," she said.

"What did you have for dinner?"

She cocked her head. "Spaghetti and meat sauce. Wilbur wasn't much of a cook. Is that important? What we ate?"

I tapped my notebook while I thought. Looking up, I asked, "Are you reading Lolita?"

Her eyes drifted off, then she said, "I left it on his nightstand, didn't I?"

"How were you and Wilbur getting along?"

"We are… *were* getting along well. Very well."

"Did anyone want to harm Wilbur?"

"He was a lovely man. No one would want to hurt him."

"What about your husband?"

"Carlos? He didn't know of Wilbur and me."

"You're sure?"

Elisa stared at me.

"Well?"

She shrugged, then shook her head. "I don't think so. He's made some comments about my 'boyfriend' lately. I thought he was just trying to make me mad. We've been fighting a lot. More than usual."

"I'd like to talk with him."

"Why?"

"You know why."

***

Carlos Rodriguez wasn't hard to find. He was at home. Elisa said he owned a small construction company but didn't have a current project. His business had struggled of late.

As he opened the door, he said, "Yes?"

I introduced myself and showed him my badge. He opened the door a bit wider and stepped back, inviting me into the house.

Carlos was nearing fifty years old and had a soft belly. He stood roughly six feet two in a pair of work boots. His skin was dark, and his face wrinkled from too much time in the sun. His hands were rough, and there was dirt under his fingernails.

I pulled my notebook from the inside of my jacket, then clicked my pen into place, making a bigger show of both actions than necessary. "Mr. Rodriguez," I said, "where were you yesterday morning about ten?"

He set his jaw and shoved his hands into the pockets of his jeans.

I waited for several moments before asking again, "Where were you?"

Carlos shrugged. "I don't remember. Probably drumming up business. Whatever I was doing, I wasn't paying attention to the clock."

"Do you know why I'm here?"

"No."

"I'm investigating a man's death."

His jaw muscles flexed, but he remained silent.

"Does the name Wilbur Pennington mean anything to you?"

A small tick occurred under his left eye.

"You know about Wilbur Pennington and your wife, don't you?"

"Who?" he asked. The small tick occurred again.

My heart raced a bit faster. "You went to his house, didn't you?"

"What are you talking about?"

"You're bigger than him," I said. "Probably stronger, too. Construction work would do that, I imagine."

He blinked several times.

"I'm guessing you knew he was smaller. You probably saw him somehow. Did you watch him before? Is that what you did?"

Another tick under his eye. "I don't know what you're talking about."

"You wanted to square off with the man, didn't you? Show him you were bigger. You hit him."

Carlos shook his head.

"You hit him," I said with as much confidence as I could muster.

His head shaking became more violent.

"How could you not? With what he was doing to your wife."

"No!" he blurted. "I never touched him." He immediately knew his mistake. He lowered his head and stared at his boots.

I pulled the radio from my belt and requested a backup deputy. My eyes remained on him, prepared for the man to fight or flee, but he did neither.

"Why don't we sit down?" I softly said.

Carlos slowly walked into the living room. The room was small and had a green sofa and a double-sized chair. Black-and-white photos of a Hispanic family hung on the pumpkin-colored wall. The images appeared to have been taken a hundred years ago.

He dropped heavily onto the couch.

"How long have you known?" I asked.

He hesitated to answer, but eventually he sighed. "A few weeks."

"How did you find out?"

"An email from him." His voice was low, resigned. "I saw it on her phone. He said he loved her. Then I searched her phone and found the email she sent back saying she loved him."

"What happened at Pennington's house?"

Carlos rubbed his hands. "It's not what you think. I only went to confront him. To tell him to leave her alone."

"How did it happen?"

"It was an accident."

"Okay, then. Convince me."

He inhaled deeply, held it, then began speaking, "When I found Pennington and my wife were …." He stared at me, not wanting to say the words. "I hoped it would stop, but it didn't."

I thought about Laura and me. I wondered if her husband had the same thoughts as Carlos Rodriguez.

"I went to tell him to leave my wife alone. I know she deserves better than me, but she is all I have."

"Did you and Pennington fight?"

Carlos shook his head. "He opened the door, and we argued. I followed him inside and told him to leave her alone. When he said he wasn't going to do that, I pushed him. That's all I did. A push." He mimed a two-handed shove. "I swear. I never hit him."

"What happened next?"

"He grabbed the phone to call the police. I took it from him before he could say anything and hung up. He yelled at me. Said I was a terrible husband who couldn't take care of a woman like Elisa. He said I didn't deserve to have her."

"What did you do then?"

Carlos lowered his head.

"What happened?" I asked, softening my voice.

"I showed him my gun and told him to leave her alone. Or else."

My heart skipped a beat. "What gun?"

Carlos pointed at a small table in the corner. "It's in there."

I pulled the drawer out from the table and saw a small .22 pistol inside. I closed the drawer and turned back to him.

"It wasn't loaded," he said. "It's not even loaded now. I wouldn't have hurt him. I only wanted to scare him into leaving my wife alone."

"What happened when you showed him the gun?"

"He yelled at me. Called me stupid. Said I deserved what I got. Then he grabbed his chest."

"Like he was having a heart attack?"

"I guess so," Carlos said with a shrug. "He stumbled around, then fell. After that, he quit moving."

"Why didn't you call for help?"

His eyes glistened. "If he was dead, Elisa wouldn't leave me."

"What did you do with the phone?"

"I wiped my fingerprints off it. I didn't want anyone to know I was there."

Carlos rubbed his hands together again as he sat quietly. I watched him, thinking of additional questions I would ask him later in a formal interview at the station.

When he stopped rubbing his hands, Carlos looked up. "Am I in trouble?"

"Yeah."

Carlos Rodriquez stared down at his work boots. "I've lost her now, for sure."

When the uniformed deputy arrived, I arrested Carlos for Second Degree Murder and advised him of his Miranda rights. A prosecuting attorney might drop it to Manslaughter, but the elements of the crime seemed to rate the higher charge.

A uniformed deputy transported him to the station while a corporal responded to the house to take photographs of the gun and bag it for evidence.

Elisa Rodriguez was about to lose both men in her life.

***

I booked Carlos into the Spokane County Jail after officially interviewing him at the station. He repeated the same version of events as he had at his home. I expected him to lie, or at least try to obscure the truth with some rationalizing, but he didn't.

Instead, he cried and told the truth. He even said he was sorry for what happened to Mr. Pennington.

He didn't even ask for a lawyer.

Booking him did not feel satisfying. It felt hollow.

I went home that night to my apartment in Browne's Addition and found Laura on my couch.

"What are you doing here?" I asked and tossed my keys on an end table.

She smiled and walked over. "I wanted to surprise you."

I thought of Wilbur and Elisa eating spaghetti and meat sauce while poor Carlos sat at home, knowing what his wife was doing.

"I can't do this anymore," I said.

"What can't you do?" Laura asked.

"It's not right. Your husband is waiting for you to come home."

Laura slipped her arms around me. She put her cheek next to mine.

"What he doesn't know—" she whispered. Her warm breath teased my ear.

I wanted to push her away and stand my ground. Words like honor and character popped into my head. For a moment, I wondered if there was a God and if he would condemn me for what I had done.

In the end, though, I ignored my concerns and kissed her.

I tried not to think of Carlos Rodriquez.

A Brother's Burden

"He's a bastard," Mick Graham said. His eyes were wild. "He needs to be put in the ground."

Todd Freeman glanced around the coffee shop, looking for anyone who might have heard his friend. No one looked in their direction.

The guy in the corner continued to drink his coffee with his head bowed over a book. The housewives huddled together on a couch were more interested in sharing a secret of their own. Behind the counter, the barista bobbed her head to something the customers couldn't hear.

Mick lowered his voice. "I want to kill him."

"That won't bring Megan back."

"You think I don't know that?"

The housewives now looked their way. Todd stared at them until they grew bored and returned to their secret.

"Check yourself," Todd whispered to his friend.

Scolded, Mick looked out the window.

A young couple walked in then with a crying baby in a carrier. The pale woman was small, and the guy looked like he'd missed his last hit of meth. He was dressed in plaid shorts with an unzipped hooded sweatshirt over a T-shirt bearing a picture of Tupac. The girl wore a white Yankees hat turned sideways on her head, baggy blue shorts, and a black Oakland Raiders T-shirt.

Todd's attention returned to Mick. His friend was a mess. His greasy hair looked like he combed it with his fingers. He hadn't shaved for days, and his clothes smelled like they'd been pulled from a hamper.

"It was an accident," Todd said.

"He was drunk."

The crying baby wailed louder, and the young couple stared at it like two dogs watching television. The guy who had been reading observed the family for a moment, then rolled his eyes and closed his book. He stood to leave. The housewives scooted closer together, their secret more important than the inconvenience of a screaming kid.

Todd leaned on the table. "The guy stopped and checked on her before calling the police. He wasn't trying to get away."

One hot night in August, Megan had gone out to walk their dog. She'd gone downtown, only a mile from their house. She crossed First Avenue when Rudy Bischoff ran over her and their dog with his BMW. He stopped immediately, called the cops, and rendered what little aid he could.

Mick shook his head. "If the guy hadn't been drunk, this would never have happened."

"Okay, fair, but you can't kill him."

"Yes, I can."

Megan died before the ambulance arrived. Rudy Bischoff was arrested and blew a .17 on the Breathalyzer, more than double the legal limit. He was charged with Vehicular Homicide and made bail after his first court appearance. The case itself was still pending, but Bischoff had hired a premiere defense attorney. The Bischoff family had generational money.

Mick glanced around the coffee shop. He seemed to think about his next words as if he were trying to put them together so they wouldn't offend. When he faced Todd again, he said, "I want your help to do it."

"No."

"Why not?" Mick's brow furrowed. "The nightmares?"

"For one."

"But this is important."

"Doesn't matter," Todd said. "I won't kill again. You once said the same thing."

Mick frowned. "That was before. This is different."

"You don't even own a gun. Me neither."

"I'll go buy one."

Todd crossed his arms. "At the store? They register those."

Mick mirrored Todd's movement. "I'll get a gun down on Sprague."

"What do you know about doing that?"

"Why do you care if you're not going to help?"

"You're my brother, and I don't want you doing something stupid."

Mick and Todd weren't brothers by birth, but rather through war. They'd served two tours in Afghanistan together. Mick returned home after a roadside bomb took his left leg. Megan was proud of the sacrifice her husband made. They had been in love since high school, and no roadside bomb was going to end that.

Six months later, Todd came back with something else missing—something inside. Todd's wife stuck around long enough to know he wasn't the same guy she married.

Mick stared into his cup of coffee. "Bischoff needs to pay for what he did."

The two men had killed together, but that was in war, under the color of the uniform and a country they both believed in. Killing a non-combatant was something entirely different—something Todd wasn't prepared to do.

"I can't do that."

Mick didn't react, but Todd was sure he knew what his friend was thinking.

"And you can't do it without me."

"The hell I can't," Mick said.

"You won't get away with it."

His friend looked up, and Todd knew by the look in Mick's eyes that he didn't care.

***

Four days later, *The Spokesman-Review* reported that a body was found in a ditch along Carnahan Road. The article mentioned it was near a dumpsite where serial killer Robert Yates had disposed of one of his victims. Yates had long ago been sentenced and imprisoned. Why that was important was lost on Todd, but the newspaper printed it, so someone thought it necessary.

According to the report, an unidentified source said the cause of death appeared to be a gunshot wound to the chest. There were no leads at the time.

The body was identified, but they were not releasing the name until the family could be notified. A couple of days later, the paper announced who had been murdered. It was Michael James Graham.

Mick to his friends.

***

"I'd like to talk with a detective," Todd said to the bored uniformed woman sitting behind the front desk of the Public Safety Building. Her salt-and-pepper hair was carelessly tied in a bun, and her skin was pale. On her upper shirt sleeves were Private stripes.

"About?"

"The murder of Michael Graham."

She raised an eyebrow. "Are you confessing?"

"No."

The woman sighed and picked up the telephone receiver. "Wait over there," she said and pointed to a bench.

Todd sat and watched as people milled about.

A few minutes later, he heard footsteps and looked up to see a man standing over his left shoulder.

"You're the one with information on the Graham case?"

The detective had a relaxed face but penetrating eyes. He wore a dark suit, white shirt, and a printed tie. His suit jacket caught behind the gun on his hip. A silver badge was clipped to his belt.

Todd stood. "That's right."

"What do you have?"

"Did you know Rudy Bischoff killed Mick's wife in a DUI accident?"

The detective pursed his lips but didn't speak.

Todd continued. "A few days before his death, Mick said he was going to kill Bischoff for that."

"So, you think there's a connection between the accident and his murder?"

"He was found in a ditch. Isn't that enough to consider?"

The detective studied him for a moment further. "Follow me."

Todd dropped in behind him, and they walked through the hallways of the police department. The detective led him through a work area of cubicles and ringing telephones to a small room with a table and two chairs, one on each side. The detective pointed at the far one, then left the room.

Todd sat and noticed the room smelled of Pine-Sol.

Soon, the detective returned with a spiral notebook and pen. He shut the door behind him, which cut them off from the noise of the outer office.

He sat across from Todd and flipped open his notebook. Without looking up, he said, "I'm Detective Higgins. You're not in custody."

"I know. I came to you. You don't think I killed him and came here to confess, do you?"

"Stranger things have happened."

Higgins jotted something into his notebook. The next several minutes were filled with questions about Todd—his birthdate, his home address, and his relationship with Mick. When Higgins had the basics, he finally asked Todd to tell his story.

Higgins wrote in his notebook as Todd spoke. The detective glanced up occasionally to ask clarifying questions. When Todd finished speaking, Higgins put down his pen and interlaced his fingers.

"What makes you think Rudy Bischoff killed your friend?"

"I don't know if he did."

Higgins frowned. "The way you talk makes it sound like you do."

Todd shrugged. "I know what Mick said. I figured it might be helpful to your investigation."

"Bischoff and his family have a good reputation."

"You sound like the newspaper."

"Still stands."

"The man ran over a woman while drunk."

The detective closed his notebook. "That doesn't mean he killed your friend."

Todd's face grew hot. "You going to talk to Bischoff about Mick?"

Higgins shrugged. "Probably."

***

Three weeks later, *The Spokesman-Review* reported that the prosecuting attorney had decided not to pursue charges against Rudy Bischoff in the Vehicular Homicide case of Megan Graham.

According to the article, the breathalyzer used on Bischoff had been proven defective in another case. Bischoff's attorney intended to challenge the results. If prior cases were any guide, the results would likely be deemed worthless.

An unnamed source close to the investigation stated the arresting officer relied too heavily on the breathalyzer results and left out important details in his report about Bischoff's behavior. That same source opined that without a factual description, the officer's reasonable suspicion of Bischoff's driving under the influence was weak at best. Bischoff's attorney confirmed he intended to challenge this point as well.

The death knell for the case seemed to come from the prosecuting attorney's own observation that Megan was in the middle of the street when the collision occurred. Had she been in a crosswalk, the decision of whether to pursue charges might have been different.

As it stood, the case against Rudy Bischoff appeared unwinnable.

The prosecuting attorney—a career politician—was apologetic in his press release but said the evidence was not there to try a successful case.

For days, it ate away at Todd until he decided to do something about it.

***

It didn't take Todd long to find where Rudy Bischoff lived. The Internet provided him with more than he expected to find.

Bischoff lived on Browne's Mountain, far south of Todd's West Central apartment. It put him on the side of town where Mick's body was found. It wasn't conclusive evidence by any stretch, but something Todd filed away in the back of his mind.

The house was a monstrous affair, and its lawn was landscaped perfectly and free of leaves. Most yards in late October begin to look rough, but Bischoff's still looked spring fresh.

It was Saturday morning, but no one moved about the neighborhood. On both sides of the house, the nearest neighbor was at least fifty yards away. Todd parked his car on the street and walked up to the front door. He rang the doorbell and waited. He did this a second time and waited a few more minutes. When he grew tired of waiting, he turned to leave.

The door opened, and a man he knew from the newspaper to be Rudy Bischoff stared back. A gun dangled by his side. "Can I help you?"

Todd's mouth felt full of cotton. The same thing happened whenever he had been on patrol in the desert. Fear sucked him dry.

"Well?" Bischoff said.

"I'm a friend of Megan Graham."

The man pointed the gun at Todd's chest. "Get out of here."

Todd stepped back but didn't turn away.

"What happened when Mick came here?"

"I don't know what you're talking about." Bischoff slammed the door shut.

***

Todd sat in his apartment and thought about his friend.

They went to Afghanistan as privates. They ended up friends solely because they shared the same hometown. It was odd for men in a unit to be from the same town, even if they were from cities like Los Angeles or Chicago. Being from Spokane made them feel special.

Mick made sergeant the week before the roadside bomb took his leg. Todd made sergeant later. By then, he no longer held aspirations of a military career.

They'd seen a lot of death there, but nothing affected Todd as badly as holding on to his friend after the explosion. The same blast killed two others. They were good men, and Todd mourned their loss. Holding Mick as he slipped into shock, not knowing if he would survive, killed something inside Todd.

That's when the nightmares started. He had them during the war. They got worse when he came home.

After Megan's death, Mick grew distant. He didn't talk as much and turned inward. Without his wife, Mick quickly wasted away, aided by his almost constant drinking. The disability paychecks would make sure he'd never run out of money, but they also allowed him to no longer participate in his life.

Todd couldn't prove Bischoff killed Mick and later dumped his body in a ditch. He had his suspicions, but they were worthless. Detective Higgins had said as much.

However, Todd did know Bischoff killed Megan and that signed Mick's death warrant. Bischoff would never spend a minute in jail because the system had failed to do its job.

Todd couldn't save Mick just like his friend couldn't save Megan. With both gone, Todd no longer had any family.

What did he have to lose now?

***

Sprague Avenue cut through the heart of Spokane and continued through the neighboring city of Spokane Valley. Just east of downtown, Sprague was home to an underworld the cops and city have tried repeatedly to chase off, stomp down, or legislate away. Every few years, the neighborhood cleaned up its act and put its best face forward. However, if anyone spent enough time along the Sprague corridor, they could eventually find whatever type of sin they wanted. It wasn't a secret, nor was it rocket science. It only took patience.

Todd walked a small section of East Sprague for over an hour before a guy walked up. He was short, with slicked-back hair and a face full of bad acne. His head swiveled constantly. He stopped in front of Todd and appraised him. Then he glanced up and down the street.

He hunched his shoulders before asking, "Whatcha need?"

Todd waited for the man to look him in the eye. When he finally did so, Todd could see something wasn't right. "Nothing," Todd said.

The man nervously shuffled from one foot to the other. "Listen, man. Whatever you want, I can get. Ain't no thing."

Todd shook his head. "No, thanks. I'm good."

"C'mon." He scanned the street again. "Everyone knows to trust Chilly."

Todd stepped back.

"I can get you whatever—"

"No."

He reached out a hand as if to touch Todd. "I know you're looking for something. Let me help—"

"No!"

Chilly's lip curled, and his eyes scanned Todd from head to toe. Then the man flicked his hand. "Fuck it," he said. "And fuck you." He pointed his finger and thumb at Todd in a fake gun.

Todd lifted his hands in mock surrender.

"That's right, fucknuts. Disrespect me. That's how I do it." Chilly nodded a couple of times, then walked off.

After his encounter with Chilly, Todd walked around Sprague for another hour before a prostitute approached. She was a six-foot-tall white woman whom Todd suspected started life as a man.

"Looking for a party?"

"No, ma'am."

"But you're looking for something."

Todd shrugged.

"Why don't you tell me what you're after, and maybe I can help you get it."

"Why would you do that?"

"A finder's fee."

Todd rubbed his chin. "A gun."

The woman eyed him coolly. "You a cop?"

"No."

"Show it to me."

"What?"

She motioned toward the front of his jeans. "Pull it out and show it to me."

"Are you for real?"

"As real as they come. If you don't pull it out, you're a cop. If you do, then we can do some business."

Todd unzipped his pants and pulled himself out. The woman looked down, nodded twice, then said, "Wait here, honey."

She was gone for almost thirty minutes. When she returned, they stepped into an alley. A battered wooden fence lined one edge, and the faded concrete of the rear of a TV repair shop lined the other. She handed Todd what he requested. As he discreetly checked out the gun, Todd said, "I wish I would have met you first."

"Changed your mind about that party?"

"Thinking about a tweaker." He told her about Chilly.

The woman sniffed dismissively. "You had some good sense to get away from that boy. He's messed up in the head. If he asks you to get in his car, say no."

When Todd was satisfied with the gun, he asked, "How much?"

"Three-fifty plus my fifty for getting it. That's the finder's fee."

Todd had a sneaking suspicion she already got a finder's fee from the seller and was now double-dipping. This wasn't the time or place for haggling, though. He tucked the gun into his waistband, then counted the money into her hand.

***

The night was cold as Todd huddled in the bushes outside Rudy Bischoff's home. He'd been there for more than an hour. His hands were shoved into the pockets of his parka, and he forced himself to ignore the cold biting at his ears and nose.

When headlights appeared, Todd pushed further back into the bushes. The garage door opened, and light flooded the driveway. A white Cadillac Escalade left the roadway and rolled slowly into the garage.

Todd abandoned his hiding spot and followed the SUV, keeping low to avoid being seen. A gym bag was slung over his shoulder, and he carried the gun.

The garage door began its descent, and the driver's door opened. Todd stood at the rear corner of the vehicle and watched Bischoff stumble out. He caught the far wall with his hand and steadied himself. "Whoa," he muttered, then laughed.

Todd approached him from behind.

The vehicle dinged a warning that keys were left in the ignition. Bischoff moved towards the back door to his house. He stopped suddenly and patted his pants pockets. "Shit," he said and turned around. He gasped when he saw Todd and the gun.

"On your knees."

"Huh?"

"Knees," Todd repeated.

Bischoff blinked several times before slowly lowering himself to the ground. "I know you. You came to my door."

"On your stomach."

The vehicle continued to warn that keys were left in the ignition.

"Itwasanaccident." Bischoff's words slurred together.

"Not her. Mick."

"Who?"

"Her husband."

"Huh?"

Todd lifted the gun further. "You killed him."

Bischoff turned his face away. "I din't."

"You did."

"I don't know what you're talking about!" Tears rolled down his cheeks.

For days, Todd had run scenarios through his head but facing Bischoff in this garage was never one. He wanted to catch the man off guard. The only possibility of getting away clean was to make it look like an accident or suicide. Todd had a rope, pills, and other items in the gym bag, but getting Bischoff to swallow something willfully or to allow a noose to be slipped around his neck seemed unlikely now.

Todd struggled for a solution. The Army had trained him to kill, not to murder.

"Please," Bischoff said between sobs. "*Please.*"

The SUV continued its annoying ding, and Todd glanced toward the vehicle.

"Lemme go. *Please.* I'll pay you."

Todd lowered his gun.

"My family has a lot of money."

"Get up." Todd tucked the gun into his waistband.

"Yeah." Bischoff stood. "We can work out a deal."

"Get in the car."

"Huh?"

"The car." His words were soft but forceful.

Bischoff's brow furrowed in confusion. "Yeah, yeah, okay."

When the man turned toward the Cadillac, Todd jumped onto his back and wrapped an arm around his throat. Bischoff struggled to break free, but Todd was stronger, sober, and knew what he was doing.

Bischoff pulled at Todd's arms. The pressure remained around the man's neck, but Todd didn't clamp hard enough for Bischoff to pass out. One thought gave him pause.

There is no turning back.

What he intended to do was wrong, but he was stuck. If he didn't go through with it, he could end up in prison for attempting to kill Bischoff. If he did go through with it, the nightmares waited for him like they had since Afghanistan. That was worse than prison because they were inside his head.

Bischoff whispered, "Whatever you want."

Todd didn't want to do this, but could he let go and walk away? Was that an option?

"It doesn't have to happen." Bischoff let go of Todd's arms. "You don't have to do this."

Todd wanted to run away.

"Lemme go," Bischoff pleaded. Like a child consoling an angry parent, he reached up and gently patted Todd's arm. "I didn't mean to do it. It was an accident."

The aroma of alcohol pushed into Todd's senses. Bischoff had been drinking and driving tonight.

"You're drunk."

"I only had one."

"You killed her, but you're still doing it."

"I can't help myself." He patted Todd's arm again. "I'm sick. It's a disease."

Bile rose in Todd's throat. His friends were dead, yet Bischoff was making himself a victim.

His arm tightened around the man's neck.

***

It was awkward lifting the man into the driver's seat. Todd expected Bischoff to regain consciousness quickly, but instead, the man snored loudly. Perhaps the alcohol caused this reaction.

When he got Bischoff into place, Todd wiped the gun down—the one he'd purchased in the alley—and placed it in the man's hand. Then he wrapped his own around Bischoff's and lifted the gun.

Both men had a finger on the trigger. Todd pulled the driver's door tight into him, trying to protect against any back spray and ensure the shooting's forensics would look as correct as possible.

Bischoff blinked slowly awake and saw Todd. He immediately sensed what was occurring and tried to pull his hand away from his head.

For several minutes, the gunshot rang in Todd's ears.

The nightmares would be back.

***

Two days later, Rudy Bischoff's son discovered his father in the garage.

The newspaper reported the case was being investigated as a homicide, but the initial call to 911 had been for a suicide. The interviewed officer stated nothing was conclusive until the investigation was complete. Bischoff's son told the reporter that his father was still despondent over the accident in which Megan was killed.

Todd's stomach hurt when he read the article. He had barely slept in the past two days. Bischoff's sobs crept into his head, creating new nightmares, and ruining the little sleep he could get. Todd hoped in vain they would go away with time, but the ones from Afghanistan had never left. He knew these new ones would be here to stay as well.

His stomach cramped further when he read the neighboring article. The police arrested a local drug addict for the murder of Michael James Graham.

Mick to his friends.

As he read, Todd's hand gripped the newspaper tighter, crinkling it.

According to the newspaper, Cyrus Jameson had a long history of criminal activity related to drugs, robbery, and assault. The story also said Mick was shot in the chest by Jameson after an illegal gun deal turned sour. A witness had come forward as an informant and ratted out Jameson.

Known on the street as Chilly, Jameson admitted to the arresting officer, "That's how I do it."

Todd's fingers ripped through the paper.

The Accident

Avery Thompson turned his late-model Jeep Grand Cherokee into his South Hill home's driveway, parked, and flicked off the engine. He rubbed his eyes with the palms of his hands and sighed. The day had taken its toll.

An early morning confrontation with an angry client had set him on edge. After that, two sales presentations had gone poorly, and his employer later voiced his dissatisfaction with Avery's lack of production.

He was an account manager for the most extensive security firm in Eastern Washington. His background got him the job, but he wasn't a natural-born salesman—far from it. He tried to grow a portfolio for the past year, but it became increasingly apparent his days at the company were numbered.

He slid out of the driver's seat as a tricked-out Honda sped by on Thirty-Eighth. On another day, Avery might have yelled at the teenage driver to slow down, but he didn't have the energy to muster much anger.

After shuffling into his Craftsman-style home, he dropped his car keys on the little table near the door and listened for movement inside the house. The usual commotion of a wife and twin seven-year-old boys was missing.

"Jennifer?" Avery called, but there was no answer.

Perhaps, he thought, she had left for a quick run to the store. He wouldn't have noticed her car missing as she usually parked inside the garage. There was too much junk on the other side for him to put his car in. However, she wouldn't have left the boys alone, and she was typically good about letting him know if she wasn't going to be home when he arrived.

He called out again, but there still wasn't a response.

Avery found her when he walked into the kitchen. Sitting on the floor with her back against a cabinet, she bowed her head and cried softly.

"Hey," Avery said and crouched near her, "what's wrong?"

Jennifer glanced up only briefly before letting her gaze return to the floor.

"Where are the boys?"

"With the Mitchells." She spoke so softly that he could barely hear her.

Avery knelt in front of his wife and held her hands. "What's going on?"

"Listen to the voice mail."

"On your cell phone?"

She shook her head and pointed to the cordless unit hanging on the wall. It seemed an oddity among their friends and family that they kept a landline. Both Jennifer and Avery thought their boys were too young for cell phones, but they wanted them to have a way to reach their friends. It was more a nod to their childhoods than the needs of their children. As it turned out, though, no one in their household ever used it.

"Who left a message?"

Jennifer shrugged.

Avery stood, grabbed the cordless phone, and pressed a button to retrieve the voicemails. There was only one saved message, and it began automatically.

"We know about the body," a male voice said. *"We know what you did. We know where you hid it."*

Avery glanced at his wife.

"We want fifty thousand to keep quiet. We'll call in two days to tell you where to deliver the money. You got two days to round up the cash. If you don't have it when we call back, we're going to the cops. Don't fuck around."

The phone beeped—the signal that the call had ended.

Using the phone's small digital screen, Avery checked the log. The caller's number had been blocked.

Carefully, almost reverently, he laid the phone on the counter. His mouth was dry, and he noticed the smell of disinfectant in the kitchen.

On the floor, Jennifer sobbed and rocked back and forth. "I'm sorry," she said. "I'm sorry." She repeated it so much and so reverently that it sounded like a mantra.

Avery sat next to her and held her hand. "It'll be okay." He hoped it sounded convincing.

Jennifer leaned her head onto his shoulder and continued to repeat, "I'm sorry."

***

Three months prior, Jennifer Thompson returned home after midnight from an evening out with her friends. She had been at a trendy bar in the Latah Creek Shopping Center.

She made too much noise when she entered the house, and Avery's eyes popped open. His training made him a light sleeper. He tensed when he heard her stumbling up the stairs.

Jennifer burst into their room and said, "I hit someone." She was drunk and hysterical, and her words were loud for this time of night. "Oh, my God, I hit someone."

Avery pushed himself out of bed and closed the bedroom door.

She grabbed his arm. "Didn't you hear me?"

"I did," he whispered. "The boys might have as well."

Jennifer covered her mouth and stared at the now-closed door.

The twins bunked down the hall. Usually, they were heavy sleepers. Avery hoped tonight would be like every other night.

"Nice and easy," he said. "Tell me what happened."

"I hit someone." She turned in circles while pulling her hair.

"With what?"

"My car. What else?"

"Did you stop? Was the person hurt?"

Jennifer shook her head but didn't stop spinning. "I kept driving. Kelly was with me." She looked up. "Kelly." That single word contained a lot of history. She was Jennifer's best friend and a woman not known for keeping secrets.

"Why didn't you stop?"

She threw her hands into the air.

"You were afraid," he said.

"I'm drunk!" She winced at the sound of her voice. She lowered her voice. "I'm drunk. Of course, I was afraid."

"What did Kelly say?"

"Nothing. She was asleep. Or at least, I think she was asleep. She had her eyes closed before it happened."

"What did she think happened?"

"I said I hit a raccoon."

He didn't like that his wife had lied, but it was a reasonable story to tell her friend—likely to have happened and hard to disprove. "She believed you?"

Jennifer plopped onto the edge of their bed. "I think so."

"You think so?"

"She didn't seem bothered by the whole thing. She said to wake her when we got to her house."

Reaching for a pair of jeans, Avery said, "Tell me everything again. Don't leave anything out. This is important."

***

The accident occurred along Hatch Road.

It took some searching, mainly since there was no moon out to aid in the hunt, but Avery finally found the body. It was an elderly man, dressed in black pajamas. The body lay facedown in the bushes and was not easily seen from the road.

Avery quickly got back into his car and drove on. He turned into the first neighborhood he came to. As he slowly passed houses likely filled with sleeping inhabitants, he thought about the situation.

He could leave the body where it was. It would undoubtedly be discovered in the daylight, which would prompt a police investigation. They would look for a hit-and-run driver, and they would announce their search through the media.

If Kelly remembered where Jennifer said she hit the raccoon, she might put everything together. If that happened, it was doubtful she could keep the secret. Kelly wouldn't tell the police—that wasn't the type of woman she was—but she *would* talk. Then someone else would inform the police.

That was too many variables for Avery. He smacked the steering wheel several times with the palm of his hand.

Why didn't his wife just call him for a ride home? She had made a bad choice, which now put their entire family at risk. He loved her more than anything, and his boys needed their mother.

It didn't take much for Avery to make up his mind. He turned his Jeep around and accelerated out of the neighborhood.

When he returned to the body, he pulled his car to the side of the road and turned off the engine. He opened the trunk and the interior immediately illuminated. It was a handy feature when unloading groceries at night, but tonight it could send him and his wife to jail. It lit him up like a guard tower spotlight shining on an escaping prisoner. He quickly lowered the door. However, the vehicle's interior remained lit.

Avery ran to the broken body and cradled it. His heart pounded, and blood rushed in his ears as he waddled as fast as he could toward the Jeep. At any moment, he expected a passing car to highlight him with their headlamps.

As small and frail as the older man seemed in death, Avery was surprised at how hard it was to move the body ten feet. Awkwardly, he lifted the trunk again. The body tumbled from his arms into the back and lay askew. Avery didn't bother repositioning it to make the older man comfortable in his permanent slumber. Instead, he slammed the trunk and hurried back to the driver's seat.

Worries of evidence and DNA and other police terms he'd learned from television shows flashed through his mind. Avery drove straight home and tried to think of what he must do to destroy proof of this moment.

After parking in his driveway, he hurried inside to grab a blanket and a shovel. There wasn't time to get anything else. In his bedroom, Jennifer remained curled up on the bed, crying and shaking.

"It's okay," he said. "I'm handling it."

They were five simple words, almost hollow, but she jumped and hugged him tightly. After several seconds, Avery broke the embrace. The dead man lying in the rear of his car wouldn't let him relax.

"I've got to go."

He drove to the Turnbull Wildlife Preserve in Cheney and pulled his car into a wooded area. He'd ridden his mountain bike several times through there before.

Avery hurried deeper into the woods and set to digging. When he finished the hole, his hands were bloodied and blistered. There wasn't anything he could do about his blood now—not out there in the wilderness. There wasn't much anyway, so he had to hope for the best.

He lifted the body and the blanket covering it, hefted it over his shoulder, and carried it to the grave. It was further than he anticipated, and he struggled until he returned to the hole. As gently as he could, Avery laid the body in the ground. Then he removed the blanket and set it to the side before filling in the grave.

On the way home, Avery pulled off the freeway at the first exit and stopped near the overpass. A homeless man leaned against a stop sign. His arm wrapped around its post like it was a long-lost friend.

Avery threw the folded blanket toward the man's feet. "Stay warm," he yelled.

The homeless man let go of the signpost and stumbled forward. When he bent to pick up the blanket, Avery accelerated away.

Once home, he went to the garage. They had too much junk piled in the spot usually reserved for a second car.

Avery collected, tossed, and threw everything he could into any available nook or cranny. Then he pulled his vehicle into the garage, closed the door, and set about carefully cleaning the trunk.

He wasn't sure he was getting all the DNA, but he would work on the problem again tomorrow. Right now, he was doing the best he could with what little light and time he had. He grabbed his shop vacuum and sucked up everything he could.

Afterward, he took the time to inspect the front end of Jennifer's Mazda. The right fender was crumpled. He searched for blood or remnants of cloth. Seeing none, he left the car where it was. There was nothing further he could do now. Afraid of leaving so much evidence in his garage, Avery reluctantly turned off the garage light.

He went to the laundry room and then stripped naked. He tossed his clothes into the washing machine and started a load. Then he tiptoed to the bathroom for a hot shower. Avery didn't dawdle, but he spent extra time cleaning himself. When he thought he was finally clean enough, he soaped himself once more.

Avery returned to his bedroom, where Jennifer slept soundly now. He climbed in next to her and wrapped an arm around his wife.

He couldn't sleep, though. His mind whirred with worry, and his hands ached badly from digging a grave.

***

They slept in the following morning as it was a Saturday.

After waking and feeding the boys, Avery checked the local news reports. One station ran a story of a missing elderly man. The older man had Alzheimer's and had walked away from his family's home in the middle of the night. According to the news, the man's health was in poor condition, and he needed medication.

Knowing the man's poor health did nothing to ease Avery's or Jennifer's guilt.

***

With her head still on Avery's shoulder as they sat in the kitchen, Jennifer asked, "How could they have found out?"

"I don't know."

"Were you followed?"

He shook his head. "Not a chance. I was careful."

They sat quietly then, and Avery replayed every step of that night. There was no way anyone could have seen him—*unless they had*.

How else could he explain the message?

Jennifer asked, "What are we going to do?"

"We wait until they call again. Then I'll take care of it."

Her body relaxed against his.

***

Two days passed slower than Avery could have imagined.

He went to work the first day, but his focus wasn't on the job. He milled around the office, made numerous half-hearted cold calls, and did his best to avoid contact with his employer.

At forty-two years old, he didn't need the job. He had retired from the Marine Corps several years before and was collecting a monthly retirement check. But he wanted to work and hated the fact he wasn't successful at this job. There were other guys with half the life experience doing double the sales volume. On other days, that might have frustrated him. This day, it barely registered.

When he was a Marine, his work felt meaningful. Early in his career, he was with Force Recon. Later, as age and duty took their toll on his body, Avery moved inside and behind a computer to collect and analyze intelligence information. Desk work was also critical, but it lacked the adrenaline and immediacy of direct action. When it came time to retire, he didn't miss the Corps as much as he thought he would.

At lunch, Avery went to the bank and removed fifty thousand from their savings account. They had received a small inheritance when Jennifer's grandmother died. Taking out the large sum of money left little behind.

The first evening passed with Avery and Jennifer barely speaking to each other. They watched a movie with the boys before silently going to bed.

On the morning of the second day, Avery called in sick to work. He sent Jennifer and the children to her mother's house in nearby Medical Lake. They would remain there until he called.

He puttered around the house then, finding small, mindless projects to occupy his time. When the phone rang shortly before ten, he jumped. He relaxed when it was his boss checking on his health.

"A flu bug," Avery lied. "I'll be better tomorrow."

"Take your time," his employer said a little too quickly. "Better you come back healthy than get others sick."

Had he been a better earner, Avery did not doubt his boss would have been pushing for him to get back into the office as quickly as possible.

The second time the phone rang, it was two in the afternoon.

"Hello?"

"Do you have the money?" The voice was male and sounded professional—as if he might have had this conversation before.

"Yes."

"Bring it to Riverside and Helena. There's an abandoned warehouse on the northeast corner."

"Okay."

"Come inside. Come alone. No fucking around. Got it?"

"Got it," Avery said. "When?"

"Now."

The line went dead.

***

Avery grew up in Spokane but left after high school to join the Marines. When he returned to the Lilac City after his career in the Corps, he barely recognized the city of his youth. The area he was going to was along the East Sprague corridor, a long-time center of prostitution, drug dealing, and various petty crimes. It was a bad set-up, and he didn't like it.

The immediacy the caller demanded delivery of the money limited his time to reconnoiter the area. He could drive through the neighborhood once, maybe twice, but any more than that would alert the caller that Avery was formulating a plan.

For the past two days, he had replayed every moment of that night several months ago. Who could have seen him? Had they seen Jennifer hit the older man? How did they find the body? How did they find them? Nothing made sense.

Avery parked his car a block away from the abandoned warehouse. Even though the August sun shone brightly that afternoon, Avery wore blue jeans, combat boots, and a T-shirt covered by a black jacket.

A Walther P99 was tucked into the back of his pants. A snub-nosed .38 was secured in a holster around his ankle. In his hand was a small backpack with fifty thousand in cash.

He walked toward the abandoned warehouse but did so from the opposite side of the street. He scanned the area, searching everywhere for a possible ambush. No one moved, and he didn't find anyone sitting inside a car. Someone may have been hiding in a nearby building, but that seemed unlikely.

Avery suspected the blackmailers were waiting inside the warehouse.

As he approached the building, a Spokane Police patrol car turned onto Riverside Avenue and headed toward him. Avery's heart, already pumping with adrenaline, went into overdrive. He fought the urge to run and instead looked straight ahead.

The police car drove slowly by, and Avery was sure the officer checked him out. After they passed each other, the patrol unit turned northbound.

Avery continued walking away from the warehouse for two more blocks until he stopped and doubled back. He rescanned the area but found no threats—just like before.

He went to the front of the warehouse, pulled open the door, and stepped inside.

It took a moment for his eyes to adjust to the low level of light. When they did, he stepped further into the open warehouse bay. Small beams of sunlight snuck in through holes in the roof, providing little illumination.

Avery walked into the center of the bay until he heard someone say, "Stop."

There were footsteps on both his left and right. He glanced each way to see two men approaching, one on each side.

"Drop the bag," the man to his right said, "then kick it to me."

After slipping from his hands, the backpack plopped onto the concrete. Avery kicked it as directed.

The man to his left continued to approach and stopped in front of Avery. He was no taller than five-seven and no more than one hundred fifty pounds. His shoulder-length hair was slicked back on the sides and top but dry in the back. He wore blue jeans and a black T-shirt. He carried a handgun in his right hand, but Avery couldn't determine the manufacturer. The smaller man's eyes widened as he studied Avery.

"It's all here," the man on the right said.

The smaller man ignored the affirmation of the amount and leaned forward slightly. "Who the hell are *you*?"

Avery cocked his head.

The man on the right said, "What?" and approached his partner.

The second man was bigger, but not by much. He stood roughly five-nine and weighed twenty pounds more than his partner. Their facial structures were similar, and Avery assumed they were related—brothers, perhaps. A Glock 22 dangled in his left hand.

The smaller man repeated his question but changed the emphasis. "Who the hell are you?"

Avery said, "You know who I am."

"You aren't Clay Magnuson," the taller one said. "He was supposed to come himself."

The brothers glanced at each other for a moment. The smaller one turned back to Avery. "What's your phone number?"

"You told me to come alone. I did as I was told."

Lifting his gun to emphasize the question, the smaller man repeated, "What's your number?"

Avery slowly said each digit of his number.

The taller brother pulled a piece of paper from his pocket. "It's the same."

The shorter one put his gun away, dug a cell phone from his pocket, and placed a call. "Hey, it's me." He nodded as the party on the other end of the call said something. "Yeah, almost, but I've got a situation here. No, no, nothing big, nothing I can't handle. Just confirm Magnuson's phone number. That's right."

The taller one held the note in front of his brother.

Avery crossed his arms over his chest but immediately realized it was the wrong move. Standing that way would slow his reaction time if anything happened, so he let his arms slide back down his body.

The smaller one shot a dirty look at his brother. "I think I got it figured out. Yeah. I'll call you back in a minute." He closed the cell phone and tucked it back into his pocket.

"What is it?" the taller one asked.

"You wrote the number wrong."

"No, I didn't."

"The last two digits are fifty-nine, not ninety-five."

The taller one stared at the paper in his hand. "Crap."

"Which leads me to ask," the shorter man said to Avery, "why are you here?"

Avery's pulse raced faster. "You got my money," he said as calmly as he could. "Leave it alone."

The smaller brother clapped his hands twice. "You got a body hiding somewhere, don't you?"

The taller one nodded in understanding. "He does, doesn't he? That's why he brought the money."

"What did you do?"

"Leave it alone," Avery said.

"No chance in hell. Maybe fifty grand was too easy for you. Maybe we should ask for more."

"I don't have it."

The smaller one pulled out his gun again and pointed it at Avery. "Give him your driver's license."

Avery removed his wallet from his back pocket and handed his driver's license to the taller one.

The two men studied the license as Avery tucked his wallet away. With his arm behind his back, Avery's hand wrapped around the pistol tucked into the waist of his jeans.

"It says your name is Avery," the smaller man said.

His brother grinned. "That's a girl's name."

They both laughed at that and didn't notice Avery's movement.

***

Avery waited until darkness to leave the warehouse. He went to Home Depot and purchased two gasoline cans.

Then he filled them at a nearby Chevron and returned to the warehouse.

Next, he collected their wallets and cell phones along with the piece of paper that had his number on it and put them into the gym bag that had his money.

He doused the bodies and splashed gas on the walls of the warehouse. He lit the fire and stuck around long enough to know that the bodies were burning.

At home, Avery shredded the piece of paper with his phone number along with the contents of the men's wallets. He added several hundred dollars to his fifty thousand and put the money aside.

In his garage, he cut the two leather wallets up with a pair of metal shears. On his way home, he had tossed the cell phones along the side of the freeway—after wiping his fingerprints from them, of course.

Outside in his garden shed, he lifted the plywood floor up. He tucked the Walther underneath before returning inside the house. He would figure out how to dispose of that gun later. He hadn't used the .38 so that could stay inside the house.

Avery put his clothes in the washing machine and took a shower. After he dressed in a clean set of clothes, he stood in the middle of the living room and stared at a picture of his wife and children. He dialed a number on his cell phone.

Jennifer picked up on the third ring. "Are you okay?" Her voice was alert and worried.

"I'm fine. It was nothing. Just a misunderstanding."

"A misunderstanding?"

"An accident, if you will."

"Oh," she said, as if not understanding what he was trying to say.

He would explain it to her later, but not tonight and not on the telephone.

"So, we can come home?"

"Yeah, baby," he said. "It's safe now. They won't be calling again."

Murder by the Roadside

Whitman County Sheriff Tom Jessup settled onto his haunches to study the body lying under the scrub brush lining Highway 195. The victim wore a brown Carhart jacket, faded denim jeans, and scuffed work boots. His skull was bashed in.

The morning sun was still low over the horizon, and the late summer heat would soon overwhelm the day.

Jessup stood and glanced up and down the highway. The crime scene was seven miles outside of Colfax. Vehicles crawled by, slowed considerably by the two local police department officers who provided traffic enforcement. Most of the cars were southbound to Pullman, the home of Washington State University. School wasn't set to start for several weeks still, but many students would be finalizing living arrangements or getting into town early.

Jessup's patrol truck was parked along the road, as was a deputy's car. A black BMW Series 3 belonging to a witness was stopped in front of Jessup's rig. The witness, a professor traveling to Spokane, had stopped for a roadside leak.

How would a body end up here? Jessup wondered. Could there have been a fight between traveling companions that forced them to stop alongside the road?

More than likely, it was dumped. It struck Jessup as a brazen location for such a thing.

Jessup returned his attention to the body. He'd know more after a forensic unit from the State Patrol arrived. His department was too small to have a crime scene investigation team, so he relied on help from the larger agency. Since the body was beside a state highway, Jessup could turn over the complete investigation to State, but he believed in handling things himself. He was a capable investigator and had solved the handful of homicides that had occurred in his time as sheriff.

"Murder by the roadside," a male voice said.

Jessup looked over his shoulder to see Deputy Rodney Howard behind him, studying the body. A tall, thin man with thick, brown hair, Howard was in his late forties and had been with the department for nearly twenty-five years. He was a rarity—a small county deputy who had never longed to work for a larger agency.

"Huh?"

"Murder by the roadside," Howard repeated. His head bobbed as if to some unheard melody.

"I heard you the first time," Jessup said, turning his attention back to the body. "Why are you stating the obvious?"

"It's a lyric from that Duran Duran song, 'Wild Boys.' It was big when we were in high school. You'd know it if you heard it. Remember listening to the radio?"

Jessup's gaze slowly returned to his deputy. "What's wrong with you, Rod?"

Howard's smile melted.

"You get the witness's info and statement?"

"I did."

"Then cut him loose. He doesn't need to spend the morning with us."

***

It took an hour for the State's forensic unit to arrive. Jessup watched as they processed the scene. The technician pulled the wallet from the front pocket of the man's jeans and handed it to the sheriff.

Jessup opened it, revealing several hundred dollars inside. He removed the driver's license and saw a picture of a serious, gray-haired man.

Donald Westman. Late sixties.

He resided in Ritzville, nearly ninety minutes north and in Adams County. Jessup copied the pertinent information into his notebook and returned the license to the wallet.

He gave the leather billfold to Howard to put into evidence for safekeeping.

***

Tom Jessup then drove north to make the notification. Ritzville was the seat for Adams County and had a population of nearly seventeen hundred people. The city sat along Interstate 90. Most travelers stopped at Ritzville's conveniently located gas stations and fast-food restaurants but rarely ventured deeper into the city or its neighborhoods.

Before heading to the Westman residence, Jessup visited the Adams County Sheriff's Office. It was professional courtesy to let a sheriff know he was in their backyard.

When Jessup walked in, there was a single deputy in the office completing paperwork. It was the noon hour, so the receptionist had probably gone for lunch. The deputy, a woman in her late twenties, looked up from her desk. She immediately recognized Jessup's uniform as a fellow law enforcement officer. The plaque on her desk read *Deputy P. Myers*.

"Can I help you?" she asked.

"Sheriff Jessup from Whitman County. Sheriff Taylor around?"

She straightened slightly. "No, sir. He's at a seminar in Spokane. Something I can help you with?"

"We found a victim of a homicide in our county this morning. He's one of your locals. I need to notify the family."

The deputy's eyebrows raised. Homicide victims were as rare in Ritzville as they were in Colfax. "Who's the victim?"

"Donald Westman."

Deputy Myers leaned back in her seat and crossed her arms. The surprise on her face was replaced with another emotion. Jessup couldn't put his finger on it, but it resembled satisfaction.

"So Westman bought it?"

Jessup tilted his head slightly, studying the deputy. "You knew him?"

Myers nodded. "Everyone knows Donald Westman. He's the town bully. He owns most of the rental real estate around here and isn't very nice about it. He's our version of Ebenezer Scrooge."

"Know anyone that would want to hurt him?"

Myers laughed. "Who wouldn't is the better question."

"That nice, huh?"

"I rented a place from him while I was going to college. When I moved out, he listed so many false charges against me that I couldn't get my security deposit back. I tried to challenge him, but he told me to take him to court. I was a kid then, driving the thirty minutes each day back and forth to school. What was I going to do? I couldn't afford to fight him. That's what he does… or did. He picked on those who couldn't stand up for themselves."

"You familiar with his family?"

"He doesn't have any. Rumor is he had a wife years ago. Never met her, but I wish I had. Would love to know what kind of woman could share a bed with a man like that. Anyway, I heard they divorced, and she left for someplace free of him."

Jessup pursed his lips while he thought.

"He does have an office, though," Myers said. "He's also got a couple employees you might want to meet." The deputy wrote an address and handed it to Jessup. "I put my number on there in case you need help, but I doubt you will. I'd imagine they'll be happy to hear Westman is dead and gone, even if it does put them out of a job."

***

Jessup drove across town to a small building on First Avenue. It was mixed in with several industrial buildings and near the town's John Deere distributor.

A bell tinkled as he opened the door to step inside. Wood paneling covered the walls, darkening the room. Photos of small buildings hung proudly.

An older woman sat behind a gray metal desk. Her silver hair was pulled tightly back, and she was make-up free. Her face pinched when she saw Jessup's uniform.

"Which one of our tenants has done something?"

"Excuse me?"

"That's the only reason we ever get a visit from the police. Some deadbeat causes trouble, then you guys visit, which means I'll have to explain it to Mr. Westman. I wish he was here so you could explain it directly. He'll just get mad at me for whatever's happened."

"I'm not here for any of your tenants," Jessup said. "I'm here because of Mr. Westman."

The woman's face relaxed. "Well, he's not in, and I'm not exactly sure where he is. He gets that way sometimes."

"He's dead," Jessup said flatly. He delivered the news cold and fast. Had she been a family member, he might have given it a bit slower and with an "I regret to inform you," but he'd learned the faster he could get bad news on the table, the quicker he could move on to other matters.

"What do you mean?"

"This morning, he was found murdered in my county."

The woman covered her mouth as her eyes widened. No tears came, though. When the immediate shock wore off, she lowered her hand.

"Know anyone who wanted to hurt him?"

She thought for a moment. "It's probably a long list, I'm afraid. Mr. Westman wasn't well-liked."

"I've heard. Anyone come to mind?"

"Not really, no. No one has threatened him with physical harm in more than a decade. He gets the occasional threats of legal action, but I would imagine most real estate investors get that. We haven't even had one of those in some time, though."

"What's your name?" Jessup asked.

"Francine Baker. Fran, I mean. You can call me Fran."

"Fran," he said with a polite smile. "I'm Sheriff Jessup from Whitman County. You can call me Tom. When I first came to town, I stopped by the sheriff's office. They said Donald didn't have any family. Is that true?"

"Yes, sir. He had a wife who he divorced, oh, it must be thirty years now. Funny how time flies, isn't it? He met her in Spokane and brought her back here. She never fit in. Big city girl in a small town. Anyway, the divorce was ugly as far as they go around here. She left in a hurry and never came back."

"Ugly how?"

"Rumor was she took up with another man. Mr. Westman discovered it and kicked her out. I guess she tried to fight him in divorce court. Who knows, since they did it in Spokane County so it wouldn't be part of town gossip. Didn't work out too well, though, did it? We're still talking about it."

Jessup thought about that for a moment. "Thirty years is a long time. He never took up with another woman?"

Fran shook her head. "When he went out of town, he would spend time with the occasional... lady friend. From what I suspect, most of them he paid. Here in town, no woman with any self-respect would give him the time of day." Fran lowered her voice. "He was a selfish, greedy bastard."

"You probably know my next question."

"Why would I work for someone who wasn't nice? Jobs are hard to come by here in Ritzville. I'm sure you know how it is. Colfax isn't much different."

Jessup nodded.

"Besides, Mr. Westman... That's funny. I'm still calling him *mister*. He insisted that's how he be addressed when customers were around. He thought it gave him an air of power and sophistication. Guess it doesn't matter anymore. Anyway, I started with Don shortly after his divorce, and I was one of the few people who could actually stand up to him. Whenever he gave me any guff, I'd tell him what I thought. There were a couple times I told him I quit. He apologized and gave me a raise both times. Wasn't that he couldn't find someone to replace me, he just didn't want to break in a new assistant."

"It's a small community to pull that kind of nonsense."

"He's been that way forever. I'm sure it got worse over the years, but we've all grown accustomed to it. After a while, everyone accepts it as part of the normal fabric of life. This news is going to make Annie happy."

"Annie?"

"My partner," Fran said. "We could get married if we wanted. Just haven't done it yet. She's been wanting me to stop working so we could do some traveling. I've kept telling her not yet. The timing wasn't right. You know what I mean? I was trying to save up another couple dollars before I actually retired. Looks like retirement was just forced upon me." Fran's eyes were soft with remorse, but it wasn't for the death of her employer.

"What were Donald's business interests?"

Fran's eyes refocused, and she nodded. "Real estate mostly. Rental homes, some commercial property, a couple apartment buildings, and some farmland he leases to operators. He also owns a convenience store, a laundromat, and a payday loan business over in Moses Lake."

"What was he doing yesterday?"

"He should have been in town. He typically checks on his properties, then gives me a list of things he wants addressed."

"We found his body on the side of the road between Colfax and Pullman. Any idea what he was doing down there?"

Fran shrugged. "Doesn't make sense. He doesn't own anything that far south."

"Does he know anyone in either Colfax or Pullman?"

She thought about it for a moment. "I mean, I suppose he could, but nobody I'm aware of."

Jessup glanced around the small office. "Deputy Meyers said there were a couple employees that worked here. You and who else?"

"Juan Mendez. He's sort of our general fix-it man."

"Where is he now?"

"Painting a house on Poplar Street." Fran wrote the address on a Post-It note and handed it to the sheriff.

As he folded the small piece of paper, Jessup asked, "What happens to Westman's estate now?"

"What do you mean?"

"He doesn't have any family, right? Does he have a will? Did he ever talk about what would happen after his death?"

She frowned. "I'm pretty sure he didn't have a will. I knew quite a bit about Mister... Don, but he never mentioned one. And he never talked about dying. I think it scared him, to be honest."

Jessup pointed at the room behind Fran. "That his office?"

"Yes."

"Mind if I take a look?"

Fran gave him a wave. "Go right ahead."

Donald Westman's office was organized neatly. He didn't have a computer on his desk, just a phone, a calendar, and a stack of papers. On the walls were photographs and drawings of old warplanes.

Jessup sat at the desk and studied the calendar. His finger found yesterday's entry, written in pencil. "Who is JP?" he called to Fran. She stood and walked into the office.

"What?"

Jessup tapped the calendar. "It says *JP, Pullman, 2pm.* Who is JP?"

"JP?"

The sheriff stood to make room for Fran. She leaned over the calendar. "I have no idea who that could be. He didn't tell me about the meeting. It would have been on my calendar if he had."

Jessup hooked his thumbs onto the edges of his pockets and studied the desk. "He doesn't have a computer?"

"That's what he has me for."

"Did he have a cell phone?"

"Yes."

"There wasn't one with him when we found the body." Fran watched Jessup as he thought.

"What about his car? What did Donald drive?"

***

A small man stood at the top of the ladder, running a paintbrush along the eave of the house. Jessup walked into the yard and called up, "Juan Mendez?"

The man looked down, his face registering confusion. "Yes?"

"Can I speak with you about Donald Westman?"

Mendez slowly nodded before descending the ladder. Standing next to the sheriff, Mendez was a head shorter than Jessup's six-foot frame.

"Something the matter with Mr. Westman?"

"He was found dead this morning."

Mendez blinked several times and then set the paint can on the ground before laying the brush across the opening. "How did it happen?"

"He was murdered."

The smaller man crossed his arms, and his eyes narrowed.

"You know anyone who would want to hurt him?"

"Mr. Westman was very good to me. I don't know why anyone would want to hurt him." His voice was even and calm.

Jessup studied Mendez. "That's a different story than others have told. I've heard he isn't well-liked."

Mendez shrugged. "I like Mr. Westman. My children like him. They call him Mr. Donald, which always makes him smile. He visits on the holidays to have tamales with us. The people who don't like him are the ones who don't follow the rules or don't give an honest day's work for an honest day's pay. If you do right by Mr. Westman, he will be good to you."

"So, no one comes to mind for wanting to hurt him?"

"No, sir. I keep my head down and do my job. That's why he likes me. I don't put my nose in the business of others."

***

Tom Jessup drove down the winding hill that lead into Colfax.

He'd grown up in the town of nearly twenty-eight hundred people and was proud of the area. He played linebacker for the combined junior/senior high school, hoping he was good enough to jump from the Colfax Bulldogs to the nearby WSU Cougars. That dream didn't work out, and instead he received a partial scholarship from Eastern Washington University, located southwest of Spokane. He never got close to starting a game the entire time he was in college. However, at the end of his four years, he had earned a degree in Criminal Justice and married Mia, a farm girl from Endicott.

Jessup liked the Spokane area and soon was employed by the Spokane Police Department. Mia didn't like the night work that he loved as a patrol officer. The pressure on their relationship increased until she became pregnant with their son, William. That's when she threatened divorce if they didn't move back to Whitman County. Jessup hated to leave a department he was happy at, but he loved his wife, and a return to his hometown held its own allure.

He parked his patrol truck alongside the station. The Sheriff's Office, which shared the same building as the county's jail, sat kitty-corner to the Colfax Police Department.

When Jessup walked inside the building, Autumn Summers looked up from her computer as she was seated at the first desk. Autumn's duties included receptionist and dispatcher, along with general information technology problem solver. "Good morning, Tom."

"Morning, kiddo."

Autumn had gone to high school with Jessup's son, who was now living in New York and barely spoke to him. She was the rare person who could make Jessup smile.

"How are things?" the sheriff asked.

"Nothing exciting except for the call this morning. Was it gruesome?"

"Gruesome?" Jessup asked as he walked over to the coffee pot. He grabbed a cup and filled it. "It was a body dumped alongside a road. If that's not how you want to go—"

"It was gruesome," Autumn muttered.

Jessup entered his small office, tossed his notebook on his desk, and sat in his chair. After a long sip of coffee, he opened the small spiral notepad and tapped the space bar on his keyboard to call his computer to life.

The door to the main office opened, and Deputy Rodney Howard walked in.

"Hiya, Autumn," he said with a smile.

She lifted a hand in response without looking in his direction.

Jessup watched Howard walk to his desk, drop into his chair, and start his computer.

For several minutes, everyone worked in silence. Soon, though, Jessup heard an irritating murmur. He looked away from his computer to watch his deputy. Howard appeared to be quietly singing. The deputy's head bobbed in rhythm as he sang, his voice growing louder.

Autumn soon turned around to also watch Howard, but the deputy didn't notice. He continued to sing as he worked.

"Rod!" the sheriff called.

Deputy Howard jumped and stopped singing. He straightened and looked at Jessup.

"The hell are you singing?"

"Nothing."

"Did you say you kissed a girl?"

"It's a Katy Perry song."

"I don't know who that is."

"She's a—"

"What is wrong with you?"

Embarrassed, Howard glanced at Autumn. She shook her head and returned her attention to her computer.

"Rod, come here."

The deputy stood and walked into Jessup's office.

"What's with the singing lately?"

"I signed up for one of those streaming services. It's where you get—"

"I know what a streaming service is," Jessup said, irritated.

Howard smiled, slightly embarrassed now. "Well, I've been listening to a ton of music lately. It's got me in a good mood, I guess."

"Well, leave it at home. The music, I mean."

Howard nodded.

The sheriff pointed at his computer. He'd pulled an AVR (All Vehicles Registered) report for Donald Westman. "Here's the pickup registered to our homicide victim. He was supposed to meet someone with the initials JP in Pullman yesterday at two p.m. Call the local P.D. and ask them to keep an eye out for this vehicle. If you have time while you're on patrol, I want you to run down there and look for it as well."

Howard pulled out his notebook and copied the license plate number. When he was done, he nodded at the sheriff and returned to his desk.

Jessup then ran two names through the NCIC database: Francine Baker and Juan Mendez. He had asked both for their particulars—proper spelling of their names, birthdays, and addresses.

Baker's record came back clean. She only had a couple of traffic infractions.

Mendez's record, however, returned mostly clean except for one glaring entry—a Voluntary Manslaughter conviction in California.

Sheriff Tom Jessup stared at the computer monitor.

***

The cell phone buzzed and woke Jessup from a dreamless sleep. The red lights on the alarm clock announced 4:55 a.m.

"Jessup," he said, his voice groggy.

"I apologize for waking you, Sheriff," Carl Woodruff, one of his night deputies, said.

"It's okay, Carl. What do you have?"

"I'm down in Pullman. Local P.D. located the truck you wanted. What do you want done with it?"

"Impound it. Don't touch it. It's part of a homicide investigation. I'll be in later to start the search warrant."

"Hey, Sheriff, I'm sorry—"

Jessup hung up without listening to Woodruff's apology. He rolled over and tried to go back to sleep. Instead, he lay in bed, his mind drifting.

First, it went to Juan Mendez and his manslaughter conviction. The only information he got so far was it occurred in La Mesa, California, roughly thirty miles north of the Mexico border. For a moment, he wondered about Mendez's immigration status. If he were here illegally, he could use that as leverage the next time he spoke to the man. He would need to verify that in the morning.

As he continued to struggle for sleep, Jessup didn't want to linger on the job's worries and pushed the thoughts away. When he found some quiet in his mind, his thoughts floated to his son, William. The two hadn't spoken in months now.

After Mia's death during his sophomore year of high school, William pulled inward. The boy and his mother had a special bond that Jessup often envied. Unfortunately, it devastated William when she died. Jessup did his best to support and love him after she was gone, but his son wasn't the same. He pushed and prodded, trying to get William to come out of his shell, yet nothing worked.

When his son started college, their connection was so badly frayed that they barely spoke even though they lived in the same house.

Jessup tossed and turned for another thirty minutes. Eventually, he angrily threw the covers back and headed toward the shower.

***

By mid-morning, Jessup finished the search warrant and rushed it to a judge for signature.

Judge Edward Pasche stood on the twelfth hole of the Palouse Ridge Golf Course, leaning on his driver as the sheriff approached in a cart. Irritation was clearly on the judge's face. For a moment, Jessup thought this wasn't a good idea. However, Pasche was on call for this exact reason, and golf was a sport Jessup did not respect.

Pasche, a portly man, wore a yellow polo shirt that strained against his belly. The front of his white visor was covered by his longish, salt and pepper hair. The judge held out his hand for the paperwork as he stepped away from the men who accompanied him.

"What's this about?" Pasche asked, not bothering to hide his annoyance.

"A murder," Jessup said and ran down the events leading to the warrant. When the judge was satisfied, he nodded and turned his attention to the small stack of papers. While Pasche read, Jessup eyed his companions.

There was a university executive, a state senator, and the head of the port authority. They eyed the sheriff uncomfortably. Jessup thought about making small talk, but he decided he hated that idea as much as being on the golf course.

After the judge signed the warrant, everyone watched quietly as Jessup climbed onto his cart and drove away.

***

Donald Westman's truck, a late model Dodge Ram, had been found in the parking lot of Western Bank. It had been towed to the impound yard for safekeeping. Jessup walked around the vehicle, studying it carefully. It looked pristine. No damage.

Jessup considered asking the State Patrol's forensic lab to dust the vehicle for fingerprints. The idea passed as he tugged on a pair of latex gloves. He pulled on the handle, and the door opened. The truck's warning chime immediately dinged. Jessup leaned around the steering wheel to see keys hanging from the ignition. Either Donald Westman had exited the vehicle, leaving the keys in the ignition, or his killer had moved the vehicle.

A cord ran from the USB charger to something under the passenger seat. Jessup walked to the other side of the truck and opened the door. He pulled on the cord, and a cell phone slid out from under the seat. He tugged the cord free from the charger slot and put the phone in his pocket.

Inside the glove box, Jessup found a loaded .38 Smith and Wesson.

***

Back at the station, Jessup dropped the bagged phone and cord on his deputy's desk, startling Rodney Howard from his report.

"Get the call history from the phone and tell me who the numbers belong to." Then Jessup laid a paper bag on the desk. Inside were the empty .38 revolver and six loose rounds. "Secure the gun in there."

Howard picked up the phone. "Yes, sir. Whose—"

"Donald Westman. Our roadside victim. Since he was meeting with someone and didn't take the gun with him, he wasn't expecting trouble. If you need help with the phone, ask Autumn."

Howard looked toward the front of the building, but Autumn didn't turn around. She lifted her hand in the air and said, "Give it to me. I'll do it."

"No," Deputy Howard said. "I got this."

Autumn dropped her hand. "Whatever. Let me know if you want me to do it."

Jessup pointed to Howard. "Call me when it's done."

***

He found Juan Mendez at the same house on Poplar Street. It was now painted, and he was up on a ladder fixing a gutter. Before arriving, Autumn had confirmed his legal status. He was naturalized prior to his conviction for manslaughter.

Jessup crossed the lawn, studying the man as he approached. Mendez noticed him coming but did not seem worried.

"You're still working on this house."

"There is much work to do," Mendez said, climbing down the ladder.

"But Westman is dead."

"Fran said to keep working." He held a screwdriver lightly in his hand. "She said we will be paid. We have to protect the houses."

"Put the screwdriver down."

Mendez looked at the tool in his hand, then tossed it on the ground near the ladder.

"When I was here last," Jessup said, "you didn't tell me about your past."

"My past?"

"Your criminal history."

"Am I required to confess my sins to every policeman?"

"It would have been helpful to know."

"But is it *required*?"

Mendez shoved his hands into his pockets.

"Take your hands out of your pockets," Jessup said.

The painter shook his head as he removed his hands and turned them palms up. "Now things are different, no? Before, you saw me as a worker, as someone you could trust. Now you see me as a criminal. It was better I did not tell you."

Jessup asked, "What happened in La Mesa?"

"A fight."

"A fight?"

Mendez nodded. "I hit a man, and he died. I went to prison for it."

"What was the fight about?"

"A woman. I was about to marry her, and he wanted her for himself."

"How long were you in prison for?"

"Three years."

"What happened to the woman?"

"I married her."

Jessup studied the man. "Where were you on Tuesday afternoon to Wednesday morning?"

"In the afternoon, I was here painting this house." Mendez pointed to the neighboring homes. "You can ask any of these people. They've seen me. I live here, Sheriff. People know me. They will tell you. And for the night, I was home with my family. If you would like to ask them, you can. But I would hope you would be more respectful than accusing their father of murder without proof."

"I didn't accuse you of murder. I asked where you were."

Mendez sighed and dropped his chin to his chest. When he finally looked at the sheriff again, he asked, "Is there anything more? I have lots of work to do."

The sheriff shook his head, and Juan Mendez climbed the ladder again and returned to repairing the gutter.

***

Jessup stood near the body, his hands on his hips. He studied the roadside and how the body was positioned.

Deputy Howard stood silently nearby, his head bobbing to some unheard beat.

"Rod?"

"Yeah?"

"What are you doing?"

"Nothing."

"Thinking about another song?"

Howard nodded.

Jessup watched him.

"'A Horse with No Name,'" Howard said.

"We're at a collision. Do you need a soundtrack?"

"I was singing silently. To myself, I mean."

"Do I need to ask the question?"

"I don't know what's wrong with me."

They were three miles north of Colfax. A motorcyclist had lost control while trying to race by a length of cars and wiped out—a single-vehicle fatality. State Patrol was the first on scene. The Whitman County Sheriff's Department was providing traffic control. Department of Transportation had quickly arrived with their warning rigs to assist. As much as the Staties irritated him, Jessup had to admit they were efficient at collision investigations.

"How far along were you with that cell phone before this came in?"

Howard thought about it. "I'd listed all the calls from the past three days. I'd just started tracking the callers when I was sent out. I turned the project over to Autumn when I left."

Jessup smiled.

"What?"

"It'll be done by the time we get back."

Howard smirked. "Why didn't you just ask her to do it?"

"Because we shouldn't rely on her for this stuff. Someday she's going to tire of hanging around us and move on to something better. Then we'll be up a creek when it comes to technological problems. We've got to start learning how to handle these issues on our own."

"Maybe we should just retire."

"Why?" Jessup asked. "We'd get fat and bored."

Howard nodded in agreement. "I can't do that. The wife likes me in the uniform."

The sheriff patted his deputy's shoulder, and the two silently watched the traffic crawl by.

His mind returned to his recent encounter with Juan Mendez. He didn't feel bad for upsetting the man. That happened in law enforcement when trying to discover the truth. He felt like he got closer to it after talking with Mendez.

He also got closer to the truth after returning to talk with Francine Baker. She confirmed she had indeed told Mendez to continue working. She had signing authority on Westman's account. Since there were tenants in place on the variety of properties the investor owned, there was a duty to take care of them. No matter who stepped in to oversee the portfolio, they would require someone to manage the day-to-day operations.

Fran then confirmed Mendez had previously been scheduled to be at the small house on Poplar for a few days of painting and general exterior upkeep. She stopped by on Tuesday to check on him to see if there was anything he needed.

Now, Jessup felt like he could remove Mendez from consideration in the murder of Donald Westman.

The sheriff's phone buzzed, bringing his thoughts back to the present. He freed it from his pocket and answered. "Jessup."

"It's Autumn. I've got that list when you're ready."

Jessup eyed Howard. "Email it to my phone."

"It automatically goes to both your phone and your computer when I email it. You know that, right?" Autumn continued laughing until she hung up.

"That kid is smart," Jessup said.

"Yeah," the deputy agreed.

"I hope she never leaves."

Howard smiled at his old friend. "You like her around because she's a connection to William."

Jessup's eyes softened. "That, too."

When the email arrived at his phone, Jessup opened the attachment and scanned the names of people Donald Westman had called. He clicked his tongue against his teeth and put his phone away.

"Anything?" Howard asked.

"We've got a decent lead."

***

Pullman, Washington, is twenty minutes south of Colfax and the largest city in Whitman County. It had grown to almost thirty thousand people on the success of the state university. The population number swelled well beyond that every school year when the students reported in.

Sheriff Jessup parked at the corner of Main and Kamiaken. Deputy Howard arrived a moment later and found a parking spot on the opposite side of the street. They met on the sidewalk under the sign for Turning Point Bikes.

Howard looked in the window before facing Jessup. "How's this a decent lead?"

"Autumn found several calls from this number. The business is owned by Two Wheel Big Deal, LLC. She searched for the owner and discovered it to be Jeremiah Pannier."

Howard nodded. "JP, two p.m."

"Right," Jessup said. Then he pointed to a nearby parking lot. "And Westman's truck was found there."

"Interesting coincidence."

"No such thing."

As they entered the store, music played through speakers hanging in the corner of the room.

Howard smiled and bobbed his head along with the tune.

Jessup pointed to the speakers. "You know who this is?"

"Green Day. They were just in town."

The sheriff shrugged.

"We're the same age, Tom. You should know these guys."

"I like country music. It's the music of America."

Howard waved off the sheriff's comment. "You weren't always such a stick in the mud. When we were in school, you liked this stuff."

Bicycles of various types lined the floor, creating a small walkway to the back of the store. Along both walls, bikes were hung, allowing for additional storage. There wasn't much unused space. If a bicycle wasn't hanging from the wall, a poster from some bike race was. The floors were original wood—the mars and imperfections adding to the appeal of the space.

A man wiping his hands with a red cloth emerged from the backroom. He stood about five foot ten and was thin with muscular legs. His dark hair was cut tight. He wore shorts, a Bianchi T-shirt, and flip-flops. The man's smile faded as he recognized the uniforms of law enforcement. "Something wrong, Officers?"

"Jeremiah Pannier?" Jessup asked.

"Yes."

"Do you know Donald Westman?"

Pannier stared at the sheriff for a moment before nodding. "Something happen?"

"He's dead."

The store owner's head dropped. "Damn it."

"What?" Jessup asked.

"I had a good sale ready that he was supposed to come back and pay for."

"What are you talking about?"

"He came down here a few days ago wanting to buy some bikes."

Jessup glanced at his deputy before returning his attention to the store owner. "He rides? I wouldn't have guessed that."

Pannier shook his head. "The bikes weren't for him. They were for the kids of one of his employees. He's buying three of the best kids' bikes I've got. I don't usually sell them. Kids' bikes, I mean, but he wanted three of them, so I figured I'd order them in. They're ready for pick up."

The store owner stepped over to three children's bikes, each with a *Sold* ticket on them. On each ticket, written in black felt pen, was the name *D. Westman*.

"Did he pay for these?"

"Not yet. He was going to when he picked them up."

"Did he say why he was buying the bikes?"

"Back-to-school presents. He talked about the kids very… *highly*."

The way Pannier said 'highly' was strange. It wasn't said sarcastically or ironically. Jessup couldn't put his finger on it.

"What do you mean by highly?" Jessup asked.

Pannier rubbed the side of his face. "I didn't mean to make that sound weird. He just seemed fond of them, is all. Like they meant a lot to him."

"Are you suggesting there was something inappropriate?"

"No," Pannier said. "Nothing like that. I would never suggest that."

"So, he was a nice guy who wanted to buy bikes for some kids?"

"That's what I've been trying to say."

"Where were you on Tuesday night through early Wednesday morning?"

"Tuesday night? At Beasley Coliseum for the Green Day concert. After that, I went home and to bed until I came here."

Howard jumped into the interview then. "How'd you like the show?"

Pannier shrugged. "It was okay."

"They were a little off, right?" Howard said. "What was your favorite song from the night?"

"'Time of Your Life.'"

The deputy's face scrunched in confusion.

"Rod," Jessup said, catching his deputy off-guard. "Let's focus here."

Howard's face relaxed, and he slowly nodded as he watched Pannier.

Jessup asked a series of further questions, but it was clear he wouldn't be able to tie Pannier to Donald Westman beyond purchasing the bicycles. Finally, he realized the interview had run its course.

"Thanks for your time," Jessup said.

Pannier sighed. "I lost a sale, but I guess it was better than the other guy."

The sheriff turned and walked out with his deputy on his heels. On the sidewalk, near his truck, Jessup studied Howard. "What are you thinking?"

"I'm not sure."

"You suspect him?"

"I don't know," the deputy said. "I need to check on something first."

***

In the morning, Deputy Howard walked into the Top Notch Cafe. He scanned the diner and found the sheriff sitting alone, eating breakfast.

Howard slid into the booth, and Jessup sat back from his plate.

"This better be good."

"Crud."

"What?"

"I forgot my notebook."

"Just tell—"

"It's in my car," Howard said, sliding out of the booth. He ran from the diner.

Jessup shook his head and returned to his breakfast. His favorite part of the meal was the hash browns, and he preferred not to eat them cold.

A couple of minutes later, Howard slid back into the booth. He then flipped open his notebook.

"What's so important you're interrupting my breakfast?"

It was then the deputy noticed the nearly empty plate. "You're almost done."

"I wasn't when you first walked in."

"This is important."

"It better be." Jessup scooped up the last forkful of hash browns.

"Remember when Pannier said he went to Beasley Coliseum for the concert?"

"Yes."

"And remember when I asked what his favorite song of the night was?"

"Again, yes."

Howard opened his notebook and put it on the table. He turned it so the sheriff could read it.

"What's that?"

"It's the setlist from the show," Howard said. "I made some calls and got it."

Jessup's brow furrowed as he read the song names. "I don't know any of these."

"That doesn't matter, does it?"

Jessup looked up at his deputy.

"He lied. They didn't play 'Good Riddance' that night."

The sheriff thought back to their meeting with Pannier. "Didn't he say the song was 'Time of Your Life'?"

"It's the same song. Regardless, I was at that concert. I was pretty sure they didn't play it. It's one of my favorites from them, and I was disappointed that we didn't hear it. Anyway, Billie Joe, that's the lead singer, he wasn't feeling well. His voice and timing were off. The show seemed a little short, and they only played one song during the encore, then bowed out. Afterward, they posted an apology on Facebook and stated he was battling the flu. I guess he ran off a few times during the show to barf. Got to give the guy credit, though; he played through most of it. They've canceled their next two shows, though."

"Why didn't you call Pannier out?"

"I wasn't sure about it then. Besides, I was distracted at the concert."

"Distracted?"

"My wife, she'd been having too good of a time that night, and I needed to escort her to the bathroom. I thought maybe I missed the song."

Jessup considered the new information. "His lying about a song doesn't prove he killed Donald Westman," he said carefully.

"But he lied, right? Why lie about something as harmless as a song?"

Jessup didn't have an answer for that.

***

Jessup drove in silence for the return trip to Ritzville, his mind wandering to various subjects. He occasionally thought about Donald Westman's murder, but he also thought about his son, William, in New York. After his mother's death, William wanted desperately to escape the small-town constraints of Colfax, and Jessup was lumped into all the negative things associated with it. That pent-up emotion continued to build through college until he graduated with an English degree and fled to the east coast without warning.

At least Autumn kept tabs on William through social media. He was now working with a theater group building sets for an Off-Broadway production. Autumn showed him the pictures he'd posted, and William seemed content. All Jessup could hope for was his son's happiness.

As he pulled off the highway, Jessup drove into a neighborhood and found a small gray house with a well-manicured lawn. A ramp led from the sidewalk to the front door. Jessup parked in front of the house. Juan Mendez stood in the doorway and studied the sheriff. After their last meeting, he hoped this would be slightly more cordial.

Jessup climbed out of his truck and politely waved at Mendez. The man tilted his head to the side, unsure of how to take the sheriff's overture.

"Can we talk?" Jessup called to him as he stepped to the edge of his lawn. Hopefully, not approaching any further would show a certain politeness.

Mendez nodded once and walked down the ramp from the house before crossing the lawn.

"Sheriff."

"Mr. Mendez, I'm sorry to bother you."

"You are not here to accuse me of killing Mr. Westman?"

"I didn't accuse you last time."

"You thought me capable."

Jessup knew there was no way to escape this rabbit hole. He had to move past it quickly. "I'm investigating a murder, Mr. Mendez. I must look at everyone."

Mendez pushed his lips together, then moved them to the side. Finally, he relaxed his face and asked, "Why are you here today, Sheriff?"

"Did Mr. Westman ever buy gifts for your family?"

Suspicion clouded Mendez's eyes. "Am I in trouble again?"

"No, you are not. I will explain in a moment. Just answer that question. Did he normally buy your family gifts?"

Mendez inhaled deeply before answering. "Mr. Westman did not normally buy gifts for people. In fact, he never gave me anything. But he occasionally brought my children things. He liked them very much. They made him smile and laugh at the things they would say to him. I was very appreciative for how Mr. Westman treated my children. Why do you ask this?"

"We have a lead, but I'm not sure how viable it is. Mr. Westman met with a man to buy your children back-to-school presents."

Mendez frowned. "Back-to-school? Are you sure?"

"Yes. That's what the man said. Why?"

"My children are homeschooled, Sheriff. Therefore, they are always in school. You can talk to my wife if you would like. What did this man say Mr. Westman was buying for my children?"

"Bicycles."

A stricken look crossed Mendez's face.

Jessup squinted at him. "What is it?"

***

Autumn Summers looked up from her desk when Jessup burst into the office. "What's wrong, Tom? You look angry."

"I know who the murderer is," Jessup said, hurrying back to his computer. "Now, I need to prove it."

Autumn stood and followed him to his office. "How can I help?"

Jessup stared at his computer as it powered up. "I need a link. Something, anything, between Donald Westman and Jeremiah Pannier."

For thirty minutes, the two of them huddled together, discussing the case. When she understood what he was looking for, Autumn nodded and went back to her desk. They both worked in silence for nearly an hour; the only noise was provided by the whir of the indoor air conditioning unit.

Finally, Autumn called out, "I found something."

"What is it?" Jessup hollered back.

Autumn walked to the sheriff's office and stood in the doorway. "Jeremiah Pannier's mother was Milly Pannier."

"And?"

"She was formerly known as Milly Westman."

***

Deputy Howard parked his car behind Jessup's truck on Kamiaken Street, around the corner from Turning Point Bikes.

When they met on the sidewalk, Howard asked, "What have you got?"

Jessup looked toward the business. "Pannier's mother was married to Donald Westman. Autumn found the divorce records. Thirty-one years ago. They divorced in Spokane, so the records were harder to find, but she did it."

"Jeremiah is Westman's son?"

"He's someone's son."

Inside the shop, music still played happily, although not as loud as before. Pannier was bent over a bike to secure a sale tag on its brake cable. He turned his head to see the two men enter his store. He stood and put his hands on his hips. His eyes moved from the sheriff to the deputy and back.

"You were at the concert on Tuesday night, right?" Jessup said. He looked to his deputy and asked, "Who was that again?"

"Green Day."

"Yeah, Green Day. You went to that concert, Jeremiah? That's what you said."

Pannier nodded.

"Do you still have your ticket from that night?"

"No. Why would I?"

"Some people collect them," the sheriff said. He glanced at Howard, who nodded in return. "What about a receipt? Got a receipt for the tickets?"

"I paid cash."

"Where'd you buy your tickets?" Jessup asked. "They should have a record of you buying, don't you think?"

"I bought them from a scalper."

Jessup rubbed his chin while he thought.

"What's this about?" Pannier asked.

"You said your favorite song was …" Jessup turned to his deputy with raised eyebrows.

"'Time of Your Life,'" Howard said. "Only its real title is 'Good Riddance.'"

Pannier crossed his arms. "What about it?"

"I was at that concert," the deputy said. "After the show, I remember being bummed they didn't play that song, but when you said it was your favorite of the night, I figured maybe I just missed it. That's what happens when you get in your forties. You start questioning everything."

"You start questioning everything," Jessup repeated.

"You know what else happens?" Howard continued. "I follow up on things that bother me. I got the setlist from that night. Want to guess what song wasn't played?"

Pannier smirked. "I'm in trouble for telling you they played a song that they didn't? I was high during the concert, so I misremembered. So what? Besides, I was nervous talking with a couple of cops. Doesn't mean anything."

Jessup stepped forward to the bikes still marked with the tags *D. Westman*. "Donald Westman was purchasing these bikes for his employee's children, correct?"

"Yeah. What about it?"

"Two of those children are severely handicapped. They'll never ride a bicycle like that."

Pannier's eyes flashed to the deputy and back to Jessup. "I only ordered what the man wanted. I can't help it if he didn't know those children."

Jessup smiled. "But he did. He went to dinner at the home of that family. Many times. He cherished those children, and they loved him. It was Westman who quietly bought the two children their motorized wheelchairs."

Pannier shrugged. "I don't know what to tell you."

"Let's cut the crap, son. Your mother was Milly Westman."

The store owner's eyes briefly widened before he softly said, "That wasn't her name."

"She was married to Donald Westman until they divorced, which forced her to leave town."

Pannier's ears reddened.

"You were the reason for that divorce, weren't you? The town rumor was that your mother had an affair, and Donald divorced her for it. You were the result of that affair, weren't you?"

"My mother didn't do that," Pannier said, his lips trembling with anger.

"Then set us straight. All we know is town gossip."

Pannier's cheeks reddened as well, but he remained silent.

"It must have been hard going through life as Milly Pannier's bastard son," Jessup said.

"Donald Westman was my father!" Pannier yelled. His hands balled into fists, and they shook. Spittle hung from his lips.

Jessup settled his weight, preparing for a fight.

"That son of a bitch got her pregnant, but he didn't want her to go through with it. I didn't fit in with his life plan. Can you imagine a guy saying that about his kid? He wanted her to get an abortion, but she wouldn't."

Pannier's eyes filled with tears. He tapped a finger on a nearby bicycle seat as he struggled to control himself.

"He created the stories and innuendo. She tried to fight back, but she wasn't from there, and no one believed her. In the end, she took the small amount of money he offered and moved to Spokane."

The red in Pannier's cheeks faded, and his breathing returned to normal.

"My whole life, she told me my father was dead. I believed that story until right before her own death from cancer. That's when she told me the truth. I didn't look him up, though. If he didn't want me, I didn't want him. He was the devil as far as I was concerned."

The sheriff and deputy remained silent as Pannier continued to speak.

"I started this bike shop after college. Been doing it for almost eight years when he called. I don't know how he found me, but he told me who he was and that he wanted to meet. I agreed, and he came down here. I don't know why I agreed to it. I should have said no. You know why he had a change of heart? He said the kids of some employee. Can you believe that? He said he loved them like they were his own." Pannier's voice shook with rage. "*Like his own*—his words."

Jessup remained silent, waiting for the rest of the story.

Pannier shook his head and let out a deep sigh.

"He said those kids helped him realize that he missed out on my life, that he should have been involved. I thought the son of a bitch was going to be apologetic, you know? Instead, he looked around my shop and said, 'I'm sorry, I let that bitch take you away from me. You could have been more than this.'"

The red returned to Pannier's face, and tears streamed down his cheeks.

"We struggled for *everything*. There was never an easy day. My mother never had another man in her life. Not after what he did to her. It broke her heart to struggle, to eke by with the bare minimum. I saw what it did to her. I knew how it wore her down. I studied in school and earned a scholarship to State. Then I busted my ass while in class. Nothing was handed to us. But I never quit, and I managed to realize my dream, to own this shop. Then he had the balls to say, 'You could have been more than this.'"

Jessup watched Pannier's eyes. There was no remorse in them when he said, "That's when I hit him with my wrench."

***

The air conditioner hummed, stirring the office air. Autumn Summers stood at a filing cabinet, tugging a piece of paper free from a file. Deputy Howard leaned over his desk, writing his portion of the arrest report. Jeremiah Pannier had been booked into the county jail.

Tom Jessup smiled inwardly for a moment as he watched his team. He lowered his head, returning his attention to his report. As Jessup continued to write, he hummed to himself. Shortly, the humming turned into soft singing. It was an old Marshall Tucker Band song, "Can't You See."

Deputy Howard bobbed his head and joined the sheriff in singing, adding a nice harmony to the song.

"Rod!"

Howard jumped in his chair and turned to look at the sheriff. "Yeah?"

"Are you singing?"

"Well… yeah," Howard looked to Autumn, who shook her head in dismay. "But I was singing with you."

"I wasn't singing."

"I thought I heard you singing."

Jessup slowly shook his head. "I do not sing."

The deputy glanced at Autumn. "Did you hear singing?"

"I didn't hear anything."

Howard shrugged. "Well, geez, Sheriff. I don't know what I heard, then."

Jessup nodded and returned his attention to his report.

"But whatever it was, we sure had a nice harmony going," the deputy said with a laugh.

Lot Lizards

Using a fork with slightly bent tongs, Lonnie Smolkowski pushed the lumpy mashed potatoes around his plate. He'd already eaten all the greasy meatloaf and most of the salty creamed corn, but he was having trouble getting the potatoes down. To him, truck stop food was pretty much the same everywhere.

Above the window next to his booth, the neon sign for Mickey's Roadside glowed bright red. Mickey's was off the Broadway exit at Interstate 90 in Spokane, Washington.

Lonnie sipped Coca-Cola from a red plastic glass and watched the patrons in the restaurant. The entire group seemed to be divided into two types—worn-out RVers or exhausted truckers. Either way, no excitement existed for him inside the establishment.

His gaze drifted outside as a door swung open on a black Kenworth. A long, bare leg dropped below the door on its way to the ground. Attached to a pair of slender, white legs was a woman in her early thirties. She wore a pair of frayed denim shorts and a tight, red T-shirt. High heels protected her feet. She had long hair that bounced when she hopped to the ground.

The woman stepped back from the truck, then swung the door shut. She moved to the front of the rig, then waved up at the driver. He returned the gesture.

She spun and headed toward the restaurant. As she walked, she massaged her mouth with her fingers. The woman pushed open the glass door to Mickey's and clicked her way to the counter. She lifted herself onto a stool and rested her arms on the bar. The server, a big guy with a jowly face and a lazy eye, moved toward her.

"Coors," she said with a southern drawl out of place in Eastern Washington.

The server left for a moment but soon returned with an empty glass and a bottle of beer. He put both on the counter and muttered something. The woman dug into her purse and tossed a crumpled bill onto the bar. The guy deftly picked it up and wandered off toward the register.

With the back of her hand, the woman pushed the empty glass away. She grabbed the bottle and lifted it to her lips. As she swallowed a mouthful of beer, she glanced over her shoulder and scanned the restaurant. A disappointed smirk grew on her lips until she locked eyes with Lonnie. The look faded and was replaced by a warm smile.

She slid off the stool and clicked over. "Hiya, handsome."

He grinned.

The woman dropped into the booth across from him and put her elbows on the table. She rested her chin in her hands, and her smile grew larger with each passing second. Finally, she asked, "What's a nice man like you doing in a joint like this?"

"What makes you think I'm nice?"

"Honey, I know men, and I can tell you're one of the nice ones. If your outfit doesn't scream nice—" He was wearing a polo shirt, khaki shorts, and sandals. "—then I don't know what does."

"Do you like nice men?"

"I adore them."

"What's your name?"

"Roxy."

He suspected it was fake. "How does a nice guy go about meeting a nice girl like you?" Lonnie already knew the answer but asking was part of the game.

"You can have me anytime you want, but it'll cost ya."

"How much?"

She named her price, and he pretended to contemplate her offer. Roxy sipped her beer, then glanced around the restaurant. When she faced him again, she asked, "Got a rig?"

He jerked his head toward the window. "That's my Chevy."

"The red pickup with the camper?"

His nod was only perceptible to her.

"Should have guessed you weren't drivin' truck. You on vacation or something?"

"Something."

"You interested?"

"What if I am?"

"Then let's go." She started to slide out of the booth.

Lonnie lifted his hand, and Roxy stopped. Her brow furrowed, and she cocked her head.

"I still gotta pay my tab."

She looked back toward the cash register. The lazy-eyed server was nowhere to be found.

"Why don't you get in the camper and get ready? The back's unlocked. Surprise me when I get there, okay?"

"Oh, Sugar," Roxy smiled seductively, "I'll surprise you all right. You can bet on that."

She slid the rest of the way out of the booth and left the restaurant. Lonnie watched her head toward the camper. Her hips rhythmically jerked as she sauntered across the lot. Without a look back, she stepped behind the trailer and disappeared.

Lonnie returned his attention to his plate and pushed those lumpy mashed potatoes around some more.

***

Thirty minutes later, Lonnie slid out of the booth and wandered over to the cash register. The lazy-eyed server saw him and walked out of the kitchen. He must have been six foot five and close to three hundred pounds.

With a slow and thick voice, he asked, "Was everythin' okay?"

"Sure," Lonnie said and handed him the meal ticket, along with several bills.

The server moved his lips as he silently counted out the change. Looking up, he glanced around the restaurant. As he did so, Lonnie wondered what it must have been like to see the world through a lazy eye. "Where's Roxy?"

"Who?"

"The girl you were talkin' to earlier."

"Oh, her." Lonnie forced an awkward smile. "I told her I wasn't interested."

"From what I hear, you probably missed out on a good time."

Lonnie shrugged. "That's not what I call a good time."

***

It took a minute to cross the parking lot, climb into the cab, and start the truck. Lonnie dropped it into gear and slowly drove by the front of the restaurant. He made it a particular point to wave goodbye to the server, who now stood near the window.

The lazy-eyed man absently waved back as he searched the parking lot.

Lonnie guided the truck to Interstate 90 and headed east. The miles and the minutes racked up until he was in Idaho. At 98.9 on the radio, he found a station that played classic rock. Jethro Tull, the Rolling Stones, and Black Sabbath kept him company during the trip.

He left the freeway at the Rathdrum exit and drove north until he found a backroad that looked like it hadn't been used in years. He eased the truck along until it came to a small clearing. Carefully, Lonnie turned the rig around and backed it up until the camper bumped some low-hanging tree branches.

With a twist of the ignition key, the engine quieted. Lonnie exited the truck and studied the area. It was quiet, and the darkness of night pushed in.

At the rear of the camper, he lightly knocked twice. The door unlocked, and he pulled it open. Inside the trailer, Cameron Pierce pointed a Desert Eagle handgun at him.

It was unnecessarily large. Lonnie tried to tell him that before, but Cameron liked his toys. Upon recognition, Cameron immediately lowered the gun.

"How's she doing?" Lonnie asked and stepped inside. He tugged the door closed and locked it.

Cameron's thumb flicked the safety on before he hid the gun inside one of the camper's cabinets. "She's fine."

On the bed was Roxy. Her hands and feet were bound with rope, and a large gag was stuffed into her mouth. Her eyes were wide with fear.

"How long has she been awake?"

Cameron sat on the bench that could be converted into a small bed. "A few minutes. She came to not long before you pulled off the main road."

"Have you already—"

Cameron shrugged. "Once, while we were on the freeway."

"I thought the camper was shaking due to some wind."

His friend laughed. "That was me."

When Lonnie moved over to the bed, Roxy struggled to pull away. He grabbed her hair and rolled her face into the covers. "Quit fighting, and I'll let you breathe."

Her body jumped, but Lonnie kept the pressure on her head.

"Quit fighting," he repeated, "and I'll let you breathe."

She finally relaxed, and he eased her head to the side. Her nostrils flared as she struggled for air. When she eventually calmed, Lonnie pulled her near but left her on her stomach.

His fingers lightly ran the length of her body. He started at her neck and worked his way to her heels. Her skin was surprisingly supple. Lonnie slapped her naked bottom, and she popped up on the bed. "She has a nice butt."

"Hell," Cameron said, "it ain't that nice."

Lonnie continued his examination and found track marks between her toes. "Did you see these?"

"No, but I figured they were there somewhere. She's not whoring for college tuition."

Lonnie rolled Roxy over. She winced when he pinched her in a soft, tender place. Cameron moved away. When Lonnie finished poking and pinching, he asked his friend, "Want another go?"

Cam nodded.

"Get to it then."

While Cameron set about his business, Lonnie stepped out of the camper. He climbed into the cab and listened to some music. The trailer shook for some time after that.

When it finally stopped, Lonnie returned to the back. His friend was tying his shoes.

"All done?"

"Yeah."

"Protection was used?"

Cameron pointed to a small trash can. "In there."

"Nothing to worry about?"

"Nothing broke. Nothing to worry about."

"Ready then?"

"Yeah," Cameron muttered.

When they grabbed hold of Roxy, she struggled as if her life depended on it. Lonnie punched her in the stomach, which took most of the fight from her. Outside, they carried her deeper into the woods and dropped her to the ground.

Cameron backed away then and left Lonnie to watch her silently. He always liked this part. It was as if they refused to understand what was happening.

A couple of minutes passed before Cameron spoke. "Mind if I go?"

Lonnie lifted a dismissive hand. His friend didn't enjoy what Lonnie did the same way Lonnie didn't care for what Cam did. That's why they worked well together. Neither of them stepped on the other's toes.

Roxy watched helplessly as Cameron hurried back to the trailer. When the door quietly closed, her gaze moved back to Lonnie.

On his belt was a hunting knife. He slid it from its sheath and showed it to her. She screamed into the gag, and her body bounced on the dirt.

Now, she finally admitted to herself the truth of the moment. This was the part Lonnie loved.

He stepped forward. "I told you I wasn't nice."

***

They left the body in the woods and headed west on I-90, doubling back over the area they had just traveled. At a Chevron station in Ritzville, they dumped her clothes.

From there, they turned south until they arrived at a rest stop near Connell, where they emptied the camper's trash can.

Around midnight, they pulled into a KOA campground outside Kennewick and got some sleep.

It had been a good day.

***

In the morning, Lonnie and Cameron had breakfast at Denny's. They both ordered a Grand Slam, but Cam's eggs were scrambled, and Lonnie's were over-easy.

"Where to now?" Cameron asked through a mouthful of eggs.

Lonnie scrunched his nose. "Let's head toward Ellensburg. Maybe we can find something interesting. If not, we'll be in Seattle tomorrow."

"Sounds like a plan."

They were both on a nine-day vacation from their jobs and personal lives. Cameron was a systems analyst for a large accounting firm in Topeka, Kansas. He was married with two boys.

Lonnie supervised a janitorial crew in Boise, Idaho. He had an ex-wife he hadn't heard from in almost a decade. Luckily for him, he didn't have any kids. He never understood how Cameron stood to have them around.

This was their third year of vacationing together. Cameron drove up from Topeka to Lonnie's house, and they headed out from there. Spokane had been their third stop along the way, but the first where they were successful.

The plan was to drive to Seattle, catch a Mariner's game, and then head home. The baseball trip was an excuse to get away. The real fun—the relaxation from their daily lives—came with the girls.

***

After leaving the KOA, they struck out at a truck stop in Pasco, Kennewick's sister city.

They headed toward Moses Lake after that. Lonnie drove while Cameron sang along to some of his country CDs. Mostly, Lonnie ignored his friend's music. He liked Trace Adkins' "I'm Tryin'," but other than that, he tuned most of it out.

A couple of miles from Ellensburg, Lonnie pulled over to the side of the freeway. Cameron hopped out of the cab and ran around to the camper. When he heard the door shut, Lonnie pulled back onto the highway and headed west.

It was almost dinner time when they pulled into the parking lot of Rowdy's Place. Lonnie backed the truck into a spot in the rear corner of the lot. Several semi-trucks had already assumed their locations for the night. The spot Lonnie chose was perfect. It hid the back of the camper from prying eyes.

Rowdy's was busy, but Lonnie grabbed an empty table along a wall decorated with pictures of big rigs. He ordered a hamburger with French fries and a Cherry Coke from an aging waitress with a wispy mustache. When she brought the food, he ate it slowly and did his best to look inviting.

It took about thirty minutes for a pale, chubby woman in a red skirt and a slouchy white T-shirt to catch his eye. She stood at the end of the counter with a glass of dark liquid near her mouth. When she saw him looking, she nodded, then strolled casually over.

"Wanna party?" Her breath was hot in his ear.

Lonnie nodded.

He watched the crowd, and some of them looked in his direction. She didn't let on that there was anyone else in the restaurant except the two of them.

"Got a rig?"

"Red pickup with the white camper."

"Let's go."

Lonnie pointed at his plate. "I need to pay the tab. The cab's unlocked."

"Want me to get a head start?"

He nodded.

She touched his shoulder. "It's your money, but don't make me wait too long. You're on the clock."

The woman left him sitting alone. Several patrons stared at him. Lonnie met their judging eyes and gave them a slow shake of his head. He picked up the remainder of his burger and proceeded to eat. It had long turned cold, but the show needed to go on.

Ten minutes passed before he went to the cashier with his meal ticket. The waitress with the wispy mustache rushed over to cash him out. She mumbled her thanks when she took his money. He dropped a couple of bills on the counter for her tip and slowly left the restaurant. No one watched him go.

Lonnie crossed the parking lot and smelled the evening's air. He hoped for something clean and refreshing. All he could make out was the aroma of diesel.

At the back of his camper, he readied his hand for a knock but stopped when he heard the shuffle of feet. He spun and stared down the length of a long knife. Behind the blade was a large man. His dirty blond hair was almost shoulder length.

"What took you so long?" he angrily whispered.

Lonnie glanced around, but no one could see the two of them. He had parked the camper there for just that reason.

"What do you want?" Lonnie asked loudly.

The man stepped in closer. "Keep it quiet. Get in the camper."

Lonnie reached up and made a big show of jiggling the doorknob.

The big man's brow furrowed. "What kinda game you playing?" He stepped back and switched the knife to his left hand. His right went to his waistband, and he tugged out a small revolver. The barrel barely extended beyond his fist. The man pointed the gun at Lonnie's stomach.

"Ellie," the big man called to the camper. When she didn't answer, the man took another step back. "What's goin' on here?"

"I don't know what you're talking about." Lonnie stepped forward.

The man lashed out, and the knife clipped Lonnie's shoulder. The pain stopped Lonnie immediately.

"Who else is in there?"

"No one."

"Open the door."

Lonnie reached up and jiggled the door handle again.

Once more, the big man sliced at Lonnie with the knife. This time, he caught Lonnie's right hand. Lonnie jumped away and saw a gash near his thumb.

"Someone else is in there. Aren't they?"

"I think there's been a mistake."

The man pointed the gun at Lonnie. "Knock on the door."

"There's no one—"

"Do it. Now."

Lonnie knocked twice on the door.

A second passed before the big man and Lonnie heard the click of the door unlocking.

"She better be all right. Or you're both dead."

Lonnie didn't answer. He was calculating a way to escape. But how does one get free of a man with both a knife and a gun?

The big man slashed at Lonnie's face, barely missing his eyes and interrupting the plans he was making.

"Open the door." The big man moved away from the camper so as not to be visible to anyone inside. "Go on."

Lonnie stepped in front of the door. He turned the handle and gently pulled it open. Cameron stood inside the camper with the Desert Eagle pointed at him. His eyes were wide with panic. Lonnie shifted his gaze to the left to signal his friend, but Cameron missed the movement.

The woman lay on the bed, naked and bound. Her eyes filled with panic.

"Ellie," the big man said from behind the door.

Neither Cameron nor Lonnie moved.

The gun shook in Cameron's hands. Lonnie's gaze moved to the left again.

"Ellie," the big man said louder.

The girl shrieked against the gag in her mouth, which caused Cameron to look back over his shoulder.

At the same time, the big man kicked Lonnie's knee, knocking him down. From the ground, Lonnie watched the man step around the door and rush into the camper. Cameron squealed as a gun fired.

Lonnie scrambled back to his feet and entered the camper. The large man was on top of his friend. He stabbed Cameron squarely in the chest, then shot him.

The Desert Eagle was on the floor, but Lonnie could only get a hasty grip on its barrel. He clubbed the man in the back of the head once. He stiffened as if surprised by the blow, so Lonnie hit him again. The big man's weight shifted, and he collapsed on top of Cameron.

As he lay still, Lonnie hit the man three more times with the gun before he got control of himself.

Ellie watched everything with horror.

Lonnie shoved the Desert Eagle into his waistband, then grabbed the other man's gun. From a drawer near the sink, he pulled out a Master Lock. Slowly, he climbed out of the camper.

After quietly closing the door, he flipped over a hasp that Cameron had installed a couple of years back. He said it was a safety measure if they ever needed to leave a girl inside the camper. Lonnie thought it was a silly idea then. Now, it seemed a fortuitous decision.

He snapped the lock in place and casually walked to the truck's cab. The engine fired up, and he scanned the parking lot. Nobody seemed to have noticed the gunshots or the fight in the camper.

That's why he always parked near the far edge of a parking lot.

After taking a deep breath to calm himself, Lonnie dropped the truck into gear and pulled away. With a push of a button, he lowered both windows and listened for sirens.

His heart rate continued to slow as he took the ramp toward the interstate.

If Cameron and the big guy weren't dead, they would be soon. Both would bleed out before Lonnie could get somewhere safe—somewhere private.

Frustrated, he hit the steering wheel with the palm of his hand. The trip was ruined, the interior of his camper was covered in blood, and he was going to have to come up with a story about Cameron's disappearance.

It took Lonnie a few miles to realize there was a bright side to things.

Ellie was still alive.

Maybe things weren't so bad after all.

The Grievance

The phone rang once and then was quiet. I lowered my book and stared at it. Hardly anyone outside of family called the landline. We'd talked about disconnecting it for years but hadn't done it yet. Someday, when it got more important, we'd do it. Until then, we'd just deal with the occasional weird call like this.

I returned my attention to my book.

"Who was that?" Jessie asked. My wife stood at the edge of the living room. She wore a see-through nightgown, the one she only wore when she demanded my attention.

I thumbed toward the phone. "It only rang once."

"I'm going to bed."

"Oh."

"Are you going to stay up?"

"I was thinking about it."

She tugged at her nightie. "Okay, but you might miss your chance."

"For?"

"If you have to ask."

I closed the book and pushed up from the recliner. "I'm not going to miss a chance for—"

The phone rang once more and was quiet again.

Jessie leaned over the phone. "The caller ID shows an unknown number."

I pulled her to me. "Don't worry about it. We've got more important things to do."

***

My cell phone rang at 2:17 a.m.

I rolled over and picked it up. "Hello?"

"Robinson?"

"Yeah."

"It's Ackerman."

"Lieutenant," I said and pushed myself up in bed. Jessie rolled over and flicked on the light.

"I hate to tell you this," Ackerman said.

"Sir?"

"It's your father."

"What happened?" I asked.

Jessie whispered, "What's going on?"

After the lieutenant told me, I said, "I'll be there in twenty minutes."

"You don't have to—" Ackerman began, but I hung up without waiting for the rest of his protest.

"Baby," Jessie said, "what's going on?"

I swept my feet off the side of the bed. "My father's been murdered."

***

Worry about getting by, and that's all you'll get.

My father told me that when I was sixteen. I had just got my first job and came home with a big grin and a chest full of pride.

He believed in an ethic of doing unto others before they did unto him. After our mother died, he preached this gospel to my brothers, my sister, and me. I was five years old when that happened.

Her death's official cause was listed as accidental, but she really died from an overdose of sleeping pills. I don't know why she chose that way out, but it affected my father. After that, he wanted us tougher and smarter than the other guy. He always said to guard your chips, as everyone wanted to take them from us. To my father, chips were things of value—something someone else would want and we had to protect. Money, possessions, and women were chips.

We all listened to my father and took his lessons to heart.

My brothers, Brian and Tony, were in prison. Brian went in for a botched robbery. Tony got life for killing a man because of a woman. My sister, Carol, went to college, married into a wealthy family, and disowned ours. No one has heard from her in years.

As for me, I listened to my father's lessons and watched how he lived his life. Then I did the opposite.

***

My father lived in the same three-bedroom house we moved into while I was in my senior year of high school. The Shadle neighborhood became rougher over the past two decades, but the house was still in decent shape.

Several patrol cars lit up the street—their emergency lights bouncing off the neighboring houses. Officers milled outside my father's home, and onlookers stood across the street.

I climbed out of my car and headed toward the house.

"Hey, Joel," someone yelled.

I turned as Officer Ken Bynum jogged toward me. When he stopped, he put his hand on my upper arm. "If there's anything I can do."

"Where's the Lieutenant?"

Bynum pointed at the house. Lieutenant Gary Ackerman stood on the front porch. He was a lean man, but his experience and demeanor created a larger-than-life presence. His dark hair was beginning to gray at the sides. I walked toward him.

"I'm sorry, Robinson."

"Thank you, sir."

"You don't have to come in."

"Yeah, I do."

Ackerman sighed heavily, then stepped aside.

In the living room lay a body. A couple of detectives leaned over it, making notes and murmuring. I stopped at the edge of the room, steeling myself for what I would see. I'd been a patrol officer for seventeen years and had seen all varieties of death. This would require something more than my experience had given me.

Lieutenant Ackerman put his hand on my shoulder.

I stepped forward to get a better view of the body. The face and most of the head were gone, victims of a large caliber bullet. Blood and torn flesh spattered the walls, ceiling, and floor.

The body's size and weight were close to my father's, but I hadn't seen him in those clothes before.

Detective Glenn Higgins straightened. "Hey, Joel. I'm sorry."

"Yeah," Detective Dallas Nash chimed in. "Me too."

I nodded at the young detectives and returned my attention to the body. It lay twisted, mostly on its back. The left arm was stuck underneath the body.

"There's no sign of a struggle," Higgins said.

"Or break-in," Nash added.

"Who found the body?"

Higgins flipped back a page in his notebook. "Bynum. One of the neighbors called nine-one-one. They reported yelling from inside the house and then the shot."

"Any suspect description?"

"No."

"Did you get the pictures yet?" I asked.

"We got 'em."

I reached down and pulled the left arm out from underneath the body.

The pinky finger was missing from an accident many years prior. It was healed and worn from time.

"Does your father have any enemies?" Higgins asked.

"A few."

"Can you think of any who would want to kill him?"

"Not really."

From the edge of the room, Lieutenant Ackerman said, "We'll work this one like it's family."

"He is family." I pointed at the body. "But that isn't my father."

Both detectives turned to me.

"What's that?" the lieutenant asked.

"That's my uncle, Lyle. I can tell by the hand."

"Then where's your father?" Higgins asked.

***

I left the crime scene and went home. Jessie met me at the front door. She was dressed in jeans and a sweatshirt. It was shortly after seven a.m.

"I'm sorry, baby," she said.

"It wasn't dad, Jess."

I recapped the early morning scene and started a pot of coffee brewing.

"Where is he?"

"No one knows."

Jessie pressed her body into my back and wrapped her arms around my waist. "Are you going to work today?"

"No. They won't let me work the case, and I don't feel like riding in a patrol car all day."

"Then what are you going to do?"

"I'm going to find my father."

***

Uncle Lyle lived in an apartment in a Browne's Addition fourplex. Officer Rodney McCrea was posted out front. We shook hands.

"That was your uncle last night?"

I nodded.

"Aw, hell, I'm sorry."

"Anybody up there now?"

"No."

"Mind if I look?"

He tapped the clipboard in his hand. "You need to sign in on the log."

"Ackerman told me to stay away from the case."

Rodney knew what I was asking and glanced around before saying, "Don't touch anything."

Uncle Lyle's apartment was clean but disorganized. It had the kind of sloppiness a bachelor developed over a lifetime—especially after being in the same place for almost thirty years.

Lyle had been in his early seventies and had never married. He had gone into the Marines after high school and went to Viet Nam. When he came home, he went to college and later opened a little grocery store in West Central. Soon, he had four stores around the city. As the big chains moved into town, Lyle sold out and put his profits into real estate.

He owned the apartment building where he lived and half a dozen other little rentals on the north side of Spokane.

Sitting on top of a short bookcase was a picture of my uncle, father, and mother. My uncle was in the middle with his arm around the others. Everyone had a smile.

I looked around for a bit longer, not finding anything useful.

***

My father retired a few years ago, so no job would miss him and no employer that could give me insight into his life.

He met every Thursday morning for coffee with a few of his friends at the Chalet Restaurant on Twenty-ninth. It was Saturday, and I didn't know how to contact those friends.

My father was also a regular at the VFW in Hillyard, but it was too early to start there.

***

Susan Meyer closed the cash register when I walked into the little café near Washington and Indiana. Her smile quickly faded. "What's wrong, buddy?"

"Can we step outside?"

She grabbed her jacket, and we walked to the rear of the small building. "What's going on, Joel?"

"Have you seen Dad?"

She lit a cigarette. "Ever since he bought that little rental, his focus hasn't been on me." My father and Susan had an on-again, off-again relationship. It had been that way for years.

I told her about Uncle Lyle.

"Do you think your father could have really killed him?"

"It looks that way, but I can't figure a reason why."

Susan flicked her cigarette with her finger, knocking its ash free. "Do you know about the history between your father and Lyle? The bad stuff, I mean."

"No."

She stared at me for a moment before saying, "This is what your father told me, so I don't know if it's one hundred percent the truth, but it is *his* side of the story."

"Go on."

"When you were young, your father was hard up for money. He lost his job with Kaiser after a fight with management. Your mom had passed by that point, and your dad was having trouble keeping up with the bills. So he went to Lyle for help. Your uncle loaned him some money but made him do things in return. Most of them were labor jobs—clean out a storage room, sweep a parking lot, those types of things. And your father would still have to repay the money."

"I didn't know that."

"Sometimes, when your uncle loaned your father money, he put financial penalties on it. If the loan payments fell behind, Lyle threatened to take your father's home."

"When did this stop?"

"After he sold the house. I guess he paid off Lyle and resolved never to borrow from him again."

I nodded. "I remember him selling that house. When I was in elementary school, I think. We moved into a two-bedroom apartment. My brothers and I shared a room. Carol got the other, and dad slept on the couch."

"He says that's when he turned things around."

"He never told me about any of this."

"Your father is a proud man, buddy. He thought he was weak for getting himself into that situation."

"He and Lyle were always friendly."

"They're brothers. Besides, your father knew he might need Lyle again someday and didn't want to burn bridges. He used to say Lyle was smarter than him, that he had figured out how to play the game better than anyone. He never faulted him for that."

***

A Doris Day song played on the radio as I walked into the Veterans of Foreign Wars Hall. The building smelled of stale smoke, although indoor smoking had been prohibited for a few years.

Behind the bar stood a silver-haired man with gray skin and sad eyes. Suspicious of a new face, he watched me as I approached.

After I introduced myself, he said to call him Willie. We shook hands.

Willie asked, "What can I get you?"

"I'm looking for my father, Cliff Robinson."

The bartender smiled. "Clifford's your father, huh? He hasn't been by today."

"When was the last time?"

"Yesterday."

"Was he alone?"

"Nah. Lyle was with him."

"How did they seem?"

Willie shrugged. "Started fine. They were toasting to Cliff's wife. He said it had been forty years since she died. Sort of a remorseful celebration, I guess you could say."

It wasn't until then I realized the significance of the previous day. I'd forgotten to call my father. "You said they started fine. What happened to change that?"

The bartender shrugged. "Don't rightly know. They got to arguing, and your Uncle Lyle said your dad wasted too many good years feeling sorry about her. I heard that plain as day. Then Cliff made a loud fuss over that. I had to tell both of them to quiet down. They called each other some names back and forth, then your father left."

"What time was that?"

"About nine o'clock."

***

I arrived home shortly after three and made a tuna fish sandwich. I hadn't eaten since the previous day, and the lack of food made me shaky. As I ate, I thought about my dad and uncle.

While I grew up, Lyle spent every holiday or significant event with us. That had continued since. Lyle never had his own family, so Dad made sure he was part of ours.

Susan's story about Dad's financial troubles and Lyle's loans was new information. Lyle had always been the businessman of the family, making investments early in his life and continuing to do so until his death.

My dad idolized Lyle's money savvy and admitted to me that was why he made the recent investment in a small rental home on Spofford Avenue. He figured it was never too late to start—

I put my sandwich down and left the house.

***

The small bungalow-style home sat just east of the West Central Community Center. The two-bedroom house was in horrible shape when Dad bought it. It had been a rental previously, and the tenants had trashed the inside. The garage out back was nearing collapse. Dad got it for a song.

His car was parked in the community center's lot.

I knocked on the front door but didn't hear anything inside.

I twisted the knob, expecting it to be locked. The door opened slightly.

"Dad?" I called. When there was no answer, I pushed the door open and stepped inside. "Dad?"

I searched the first bedroom but didn't find him. I walked through the kitchen, the second bedroom, and the bathroom before heading to the basement. He was seated in the corner, a blanket around his shoulders.

"Hey, Sport," he said, his voice soft. His skin was pale, and his eyes were red from crying.

I sat on the concrete floor in the opposite corner of the small basement room. "What's going on?"

"Did you find Lyle?"

"We found him."

"What I did was wrong."

"What happened?"

Tears welled in his eyes and streamed down his cheeks. "It was forty years ago your mother left me."

"I know, Dad. I'm sorry I didn't call."

He closed his eyes and shook his head. "He told me I was a fool for loving her all these years."

"Why would he say that?"

"He was drunk."

Lyle's drinking got progressively worse over the years.

My dad wiped his eyes with the blanket, his hands still hidden by the fabric. "He told me they had an affair."

I stared at my father, not knowing the right words to say.

"He said it wasn't serious. Just an occasional get-together." He choked up and fought to control his tears.

"Do you think— Was Lyle telling the truth?"

Dad nodded. "After your mother's death, they performed an autopsy. They found—" He looked away before saying, "She was pregnant."

I wrapped my arms around my knees and watched my father.

"We had four kids and agreed it was time to stop, so I had a vasectomy after you were born."

I lowered my head.

"After learning that, I figured she took her life to avoid admitting what she had done. I still loved her and would have forgiven her. I wish I could have told her that."

He cried softly for a couple of minutes.

"I couldn't forgive Lyle for it, though. He laughed at me for being weak over her. Even when I got my gun, he laughed. He said there was no way I would go through with it. After I did it, I left the house. I tried calling you from a payphone, but I could only remember your old number. I hung up before you or Jess could answer. I was afraid to tell you guys what I did."

"Where's the gun, Dad?"

The weapon slid out from underneath the blanket. His hand covered it.

"Push it to me, Dad."

"I was going to end it here."

"You don't want to do that."

"I miss your mom."

"I know."

"I never stopped loving her."

"I know that, too. I'll stand by you through this."

Tears streamed down his face, and his hand clenched the gun.

"I love you, Dad. Now, push the gun to me."

He lowered his head and cried. When he finally looked up, he wasn't the same man who preached about being tougher than the other guy. The defeat in his eyes scared me more than anything I'd ever seen on the street.

"I love you, Sport," he said.

With a twist of his hand, he slid the gun to me.

Loyalty Lost

Scalding coffee burned Seth Larsen's tongue, and he violently shook his head in hopes of lessening the pain. He couldn't speak since it hurt so much.

Nearby, Todd Rafferty laughed at his partner's discomfort.

Larsen stomped his foot repeatedly until he finally managed to swallow. "Shit," he muttered before sticking his tongue into the crisp air.

Rafferty sipped from his coffee, then said, "Should have put ice in it like I told you."

The two police officers stood outside in the cold January night, enjoying the clear sky and the tenth straight day with no new snow. Their patrol car idled as they leaned against the warm front end.

Above them, the illuminated Fuel & Go sign hummed and clicked as it flickered. A stiff breeze blew through the parking lot and sent a used coffee cup tumbling by.

Both men stood slightly taller than six feet due to combat boots. Larsen's dark hair was cut in a military high and tight. Rafferty's sandy hair was short and spiked with hair gel. Larsen was thirty-five, a year older than his friend. Each wore department-issued coats over their dark blue uniforms with turtlenecks underneath their body armor.

Rafferty pulled a pack of Marlboro Lights from a pocket and shook a cigarette loose. He lit it with a scratched, silver Zippo. Rafferty proudly carried the lighter since leaving the Army almost twelve years ago.

He'd told Larsen several times how he thought the Zippo was his good luck charm after making it through several war zones.

Following a long, slow exhale, Rafferty asked, "How's the new team?"

Larsen shrugged. "Marginal, at best. Couple carnivores, but the rest of them are paste-eating window-lickers."

Rafferty took another drag from his cigarette.

Larsen shook his head. "I can't believe we're not working together this year."

"Politics." Rafferty spat on the ground.

The two men had been on the same patrol team for the past three years. That all changed a couple of weeks before the start of the new roster.

Every November, the department sent out bid sheets so each officer could select the team they wanted. When the brass reviewed the bids, they gave preference by hire date.

"Seniority has priority," the old bulls said. The young guys didn't get much choice, but Rafferty and Larsen had been around eight years, which meant they had enough juice to get the same graveyard team. Maybe not day shift or even swing, but not many guys with their time on wanted to work nights.

This year, however, the department put the two friends on graveyard but assigned them to different teams. This move occurred only days before the rotation changed. As a result, Larsen worked the graveyard shift on Tuesday through Friday, while Rafferty worked the same shift Friday through Monday. That meant for the next year, the men would only work one night a week together—Friday. It was a bitter pill for the longtime partners to swallow.

"We should have filed a grievance," Larsen said as he considered whether to take another drink of the scalding coffee.

Rafferty waved his cigarette in the air; its cherry ember left streaks in the darkness. "Let's not make a stink about it."

"Why not? The bastards ignored the shift bid. They can't move you at the last minute."

"They can do whatever they want. Besides, I've got an IA complaint,"

Larsen eyed his friend. "You got beefed? For what?"

"Doesn't matter. Right now, I don't want to piss off the union or the administration."

"No, seriously. What happened?"

Rafferty dropped his cigarette to the asphalt and ground it out with the toe of his boot. "When you were off for vacation, I arrested some chick who accused me of groping her while in cuffs."

Larsen's mouth dropped open. "And the department believes her?"

A smirk crossed Rafferty's lips. "The girl's got her mom corroborating the story. They've set it up nicely. I've got to mind my Ps and Qs until this gets resolved."

Larsen studied his friend as he absently lifted the coffee to his lips. Just before he sipped, he realized what he was doing. He pulled the cup back from his mouth and asked, "Did you do it?"

Rafferty clucked his tongue against the roof of his mouth. "The girl was a skank. If I was going to feel anyone up, I would have picked better. Hell, I would have accosted her mother before her."

"So, we let the administration get away with splitting us up?"

Rafferty shrugged. "You know I love ya, brother, but I've got my career to worry about."

Larsen leaned against the car and looked up at the convenience store's blinking sign.

Rafferty punched his friend's arm. "Why are you worried? I'm the one with the complaint."

"But it's ruined our year."

"Our year isn't ruined," Rafferty said with a chuckle. "We still have Friday nights."

They sipped their coffees then and watched the passing traffic on Clearwater Avenue until dispatch sent them on another call.

***

The next night, Saturday, Seth Larsen took his wife, Lacey, out for their anniversary. At his wife's request, they went to Wasabi Wow, a new sushi restaurant that overlooked the Columbia River.

Seth watched Lacey read the menu. Even after years of marriage, she still fascinated him. She was a petite woman, barely five-four and a hundred ten pounds. Her long ginger hair was pushed behind her shoulders and looked radiant against her black turtleneck.

Lacey would turn thirty-three in March and was as beautiful as the first day he met her. She worked at Mindscape, an independent bookstore only a few blocks from the sushi restaurant where they now sat. Seth knew it was a cliché, but he told everyone that Lacey took his breath away the first time he saw her.

The truth was, she continued to take his breath away, and he still couldn't believe she had agreed to spend her life with him.

It took almost a year of dating before Seth got up the nerve to ask Lacey to be his wife. Their wedding day was exactly four years ago.

They were eating an order of spicy tuna rolls and drinking Asahi when Lacey asked how Todd was doing.

"He likes his new team—more than I like mine."

"Are you guys going to file a grievance with the union?"

Seth picked up a roll with his chopsticks and dipped it into a slurry of soy sauce and wasabi. "He asked me not to."

Lacey tilted her head, a silent question.

Seth stuffed the roll into his mouth and chewed before answering. After his mouth was empty, he laid out the story for her. When he finished, Lacey shook her head in disbelief.

"Doesn't sound like Todd."

"It's bullshit. There's no way that accusation will stick, but until the investigation is over, he doesn't want to stir the pot. Can't say as I blame him."

Lacey studied her husband's face, and a small smile formed on her lips.

"What?"

She shook her head. "Huh?"

"Why were you were smiling?"

"Because you're so cute when you worry about your friend."

***

The following Friday night, Rafferty and Larsen rode together on their shift. The week had been a rough one for Larsen. Wednesday and Thursday had both gone long, with late arrests and hours of paperwork. He thought the overtime pay would be nice, but the workload had drained him by the end of the week.

Around four in the morning, the two men stopped at the Fuel & Go on Clearwater for their morning coffee ritual. The night had raced by after a burglary arrest, a quick foot-pursuit, and a fight. Once the bars closed, though, the police radio went almost silent.

After buying coffee, they returned to the car so Rafferty could smoke. He shook a cigarette loose from the pack and stuck it in his mouth. He then opened a book of matches, pulled one free, and lit it with a snap. A breeze picked up and extinguished the flame. "Damn it," he muttered. He then tugged another match free, lit it, and started his cigarette. He flicked the match away and leaned against the patrol car.

"How's the IA coming?" Larsen asked.

Rafferty shrugged and inhaled on his cigarette.

"You think they're going to dismiss it?"

"Probably. It'll just take time. You know how it is."

Larsen swirled the coffee in his cup. He put a couple of cubes of ice in it tonight. "Anything new come up?"

"No." Rafferty stared straight ahead.

"I can check into this woman if you want. See if we can find any dirt on her."

Rafferty turned to Larsen. "Leave it alone."

"But I want to help."

"Help me by not doing anything. Don't say anything to anyone. I want to keep this as quiet as possible." Something flashed in Rafferty's eyes that reminded Larsen of fear.

Not really understanding his friend's request, Larsen said, "Okay, I'll leave it alone."

Rafferty flicked his cigarette away. "Let's get back to work."

***

The next afternoon, Seth Larsen awoke with his body tired from the long workweek, but his mind happy for the start of his weekend. Lacey moved carefully around the house, trying hard not to wake him. Seth sat upright in bed, rubbed the sleep from his eyes, and blinked at the sunlight sneaking in between the blackout curtains.

When he stood, Seth grabbed the jeans Lacey put on the arm of the recliner that sat near the small television. The chair had belonged to her father, and she liked keeping it in their bedroom. She would sit in it and watch tv on those nights Seth worked.

Lacey had a habit of picking up any pants or shirts he left on the floor and placing them over the recliner's arm. When Seth lifted the jeans, a handful of change slipped out of the pockets. The coins dropped onto the chair and alongside the seat cushion.

He stepped into the Levi's and buttoned them before digging into the recliner for the lost coins. His fingers wrapped around something small and hard. When he pulled it free, he stared at it for several seconds, trying to figure out how it ended up in the chair.

His stomach cramped when he finally put the pieces together, and he fought back the urge to vomit. He walked into the bathroom and locked the door.

Seth Larsen sat on the toilet seat lid and stared at the little silver lighter with its years of scratch marks.

When Larsen returned to work on Tuesday, he did very little. He did his best to avoid calls for service and didn't initiate a single contact.

The discovery of the Zippo lighter plagued him. He alternated between reality and fantasy.

Maybe finding the lighter was the result of something harmless. Rafferty could have stopped by the house and talked with his wife about throwing him a surprise birthday party. Larsen's birthday was in another month, so it was a plausible argument.

Or perhaps the Zippo was his late father-in-law's, and Larsen just discovered it now. A lot of those lighters look alike.

Maybe this was a giant prank, and the three of them would laugh it off over a couple of beers.

Or perhaps it was just as he thought—his friend was sleeping with his wife.

That night crept by in a haze of self-doubt and sadness.

His supervisor rejected two of his reports for lack of focus and poor investigative technique. Larsen rewrote the narratives as ordered, but his mind never abandoned the hurt he felt.

On Wednesday night, while still on patrol, Larsen left Kennewick for the nearby city of West Richland. His house was at the end of the cul-de-sac on Mockingbird Court. The four-bedroom house stood proudly with its front yard and driveway under a skiff of snow that had fallen hours earlier. There was no light on inside the house.

In the driveway, a black Honda—Lacey's car—sat alone. Larsen was relieved until he noticed the footprints in the small amount of snow that led from the street up to the house. He tried to find their origin, but they were lost in the middle of the road due to tire marks. Larsen turned his patrol car around and slowly drove from his neighborhood. A block away, he found it—a red Silverado with a Marine Corps sticker in the back window. He didn't need to run the license plate to know the truck belonged to his best friend.

***

Seth Larsen awoke on Thursday, dressed without showering, and drove into the department around noon. It took him about thirty minutes to find Dave Beckwith, the union vice-president. He and Beckwith had gone to the academy together and kept close over the years.

Larsen asked Beckwith to lunch. Being one never to turn away a free sandwich, the man accepted. The two of them walked a couple of blocks over to Dagwood, a deli based on *Blondie's* comic strip. It was a tiny spot, with a long counter and several tables packed next to each other.

They chatted about union business, family happenings, and then department gossip. During a lull in the conversation, Larsen asked him what he thought about Rafferty's investigation.

"Investigation?" Beckwith smirked. "What are you talking about?"

"The IA Todd's got."

"Rafferty's got a cleaner record than you."

Larsen forced a smile. "That's good," he lied.

Beckwith pushed his empty plate aside. He had polished off his Reuben sandwich while most of Larsen's lunch remained untouched.

"What led you to believe there was an investigation?"

Larsen waved his hand dismissively. "I overheard a couple of guys talking, and I thought they mentioned Todd. I must have misheard the name."

Beckwith played with the straw in his Pepsi. "Can I ask you something?"

"Sure," Larsen said and poked his sandwich with his fork.

"Why did Rafferty ask to be switched to a new team at the last minute?"

Larsen quit poking his sandwich and looked up. "*He* asked? I thought the brass moved him."

"No," Beckwith said, "It was Rafferty's request. I thought it was strange when he asked, but he got one of the guys on your team now to switch with him, so we didn't have a problem with it."

Larsen rubbed his face. "I have no idea why he would want to be on a different team," he said.

The lie turned his stomach.

***

When Friday rolled around, Seth Larsen could barely keep himself together. Before the shift, he cried in his car and couldn't stop for nearly ten minutes. He parked behind a burnt-out warehouse and sobbed until no more tears came.

Lacey was everything to him, and he couldn't stand the thought of losing her. He punched his steering wheel, imagining it was the face of his former partner. The horn beeped with each punch. When Larsen finally got control of himself, he drove into the station.

Todd Rafferty walked into the roll call room, all smile and swagger. He patted Larsen on the back, "Hey, man, how was the week?"

Larsen shrugged and looked around the room, afraid to make eye contact which might start the tears again. The old fluorescent lights in the room cast a yellowish glow. Larsen usually ignored the lights, but they made him feel queasy now.

"Want to double up tonight?" Rafferty asked.

Larsen absently nodded.

"You okay?"

"Yeah. Sorry. Got some stuff on my mind."

Rafferty made small talk then, and Larsen grunted or nodded at the appropriate times.

Larsen almost chickened out and told Rafferty he wanted to ride alone, but he didn't. Doing that would have led to questions he didn't want to answer and a conversation he didn't want to have.

When roll call was over, they hit the streets.

He considered confronting Rafferty during the shift but couldn't convince himself to go through with it. He wanted to talk to Lacey first, to make sure he said the right things, and tell her that he would always love her, no matter what happened between her and Rafferty. But he already chickened out several times this week when it came to talking with her.

Confronting Rafferty now would only complicate what he wanted to say to his wife.

As they responded to various calls, Larsen's thumb absently rubbed the Zippo he now kept in his pocket.

Around three in the morning, they stopped again at their favorite convenience store. Both men brought their coffees out into the cold night air. Rafferty removed a cigarette and lit it with a plastic Bic lighter.

"What happened to your Zippo?" Larsen asked. His hand gripped the hunk of metal in his pocket.

Rafferty shrugged and sucked on the cigarette. "Lost it." Small puffs of smoke escaped from his mouth as he spoke.

Larsen looked away. He wanted to yank the lighter from his pocket and shove it into his friend's face. Instead, Larsen stood there as his stomach cramps worsened. He winced in pain and bent slightly over.

"What's wrong?"

"Stomach's bothering me."

Rafferty tossed his cigarette away. "Want to go back to the station or something?"

"I'm fine."

"You sure? You've been acting kind of strange tonight."

"I'm fine," Larsen snapped.

Rafferty stepped back. "What's up with you?"

Venomous words entered Larsen's mouth. Before he could spit them out, a piercing tone came through both of their portable radios. As soon as the noise ended, a woman announced, "*Hold-up alarm at Riverway Stop and Shop on Fourth Avenue.*"

Larsen and Rafferty dropped their cups of coffee on the ground and dove into their patrol car. Rafferty slipped the car into gear, and the tires squealed in protest as they raced out of the parking lot.

The radio squawked before the dispatcher's smooth voice came over the air again.

"*Suspect is described as a white male, mid-thirties, six-foot, with blue jeans and a black coat. Suspect is armed, I*

Their patrol car sped along Clearwater Avenue before zigzagging to Fourth. Larsen clutched his stomach while they drove toward the scene. Rafferty frowned as he concentrated on driving.

As they got closer to the convenience store, Rafferty slowed the car. Both men scanned the area, their heads swiveling back and forth, looking for someone matching the suspect's description.

Movement caught Larsen's eye. A figure in blue jeans and a black jacket dashed behind Westgate Elementary School, which sat west of the convenience store. "There," Larsen yelled and pointed.

Rafferty pushed the accelerator to the floor, and the car lurched forward.

Larsen snatched the microphone from its bracket. After announcing his callsign, he said, "We've got a suspect matching that description. He's running north behind Westgate Elementary."

When he put the microphone back, several other officers chimed in that they were headed to that location.

Rafferty pointed the car toward where the figure had run. The vehicle raced across the school parking lot, gaining speed.

"Watch out," Larsen yelled, and Rafferty cranked the steering wheel to the right just as the car hit a concrete parking block.

The left front wheel folded under the patrol car, and they skidded to a stop. Both men jumped out of the vehicle with their guns drawn. With only a nod for communication, Rafferty and Larsen split up. Rafferty ran after the suspect, and Larsen headed toward the opposite side of the building.

Larsen rounded the first corner, his legs pounding the concrete. He slowed as he approached another corner. He lifted his gun and carefully peered out.

At the rear of the building, the suspect was on one knee with his back to Larsen. In his hand was a gun.

Larsen opened his mouth, but he remained silent. He leveled his weapon at the suspect; the trigger teased his finger.

Movement from the far end of the school seemed to catch the suspect's eye. His body tensed, he leaned slightly forward, and he extended his gun.

Larsen's gaze went to the movement as well.

With his Glock in his hand, Rafferty crept along the rear of the building. In the darkness ahead of him, he seemed to notice a silent figure kneeling on the ground.

"Seth?" he called.

A gun fired.

***

A week passed.

Interviews and well-wishers filled the hours and days. Seth Larsen quickly grew sick of answering questions and dutifully acknowledging the glances from other officers.

He stared straight ahead, his thoughts still twisting around that night.

To his right, Chief of Police Hammond sat, his head bowed in silent reflection. He was a slim man with short, dark hair and a wispy mustache. To his left was Lacey, her hand clutching tightly to his as tears worked their way down her cheeks.

The church was a hum of activity as officers, friends, and family filed in, grabbing a seat on one of the pews for a better look at the casket of Todd Rafferty.

Larsen ignored the casket and the body of his former friend. His stomach cramped, and he winced as he struggled to ignore the pain.

The chief leaned over. "Just to let you know," he whispered, "as soon as the shooting review board comes back with a clean pass, you'll be awarded a Silver Star."

Larsen lowered his head. Silver Stars were awarded for bravery above and beyond the call of duty, not for what he did. His stomach cramped again.

The chief saw Larsen flinch from the pain in his gut. "You okay, son?"

He whispered, "Stomach's been bothering me since that night."

"It'll get better." The chief grasped his shoulder. "Just remember, you did the right thing."

Larsen looked forward as the pastor entered the church. Everyone rose. After the pastor walked to the podium, he lifted his arms. "Ladies and gentlemen, please be seated."

Lacey cried softly next to him and squeezed his hand. He leaned over and put his lips near her ear. The words caught in his throat. "I love you more than you will ever know."

The tears came faster now as she turned and lightly kissed him on the lips. Her blue eyes focused on his. "I love you."

Larsen gently wiped the tears from her face before turning his attention back to the pastor. In a few minutes, Larsen would be asked to give the eulogy for his former partner. He tried to avoid the responsibility but, in the end, he relented. He figured he would come up with something appropriate to say when the time came.

"Let us pray," the pastor said, and the church fell silent.

As the pastor bowed his head, Seth Larsen stuck his hand into his pocket and rubbed the Zippo lighter hidden within.

Whisper

She watched him dig his wallet from his back pocket. When he finally tugged it free, he smiled awkwardly and patted her hip. She wore a tattered black robe that stopped just below her butt. He didn't try to go under the garment to cop another feel—he wasn't paying for that and likely knew better than to try.

"Always a good time, Whisper."

Tawny crossed her arms, pretended to smile, and watched the heavyset man.

She didn't mind him using her nickname. For the past couple of years, she'd begun introducing herself as such. Before that, she'd used her street name for so long she'd almost forgotten her birth name.

Alton Summerset was in his mid-fifties, short and chubby, but a fancy dresser. His suits appeared to be handmade. Although his hair was thinning, it was always nicely trimmed. He sweated terribly in bed and was horrible at the act, but he smelled nice and used mouthwash. In her profession, she looked for the good where she could find it.

He pulled five bills from the leather wallet and held them out. It was a dirty power play, to make her come and take them, but everyone had their kinks—the little games they played with her. Tawny stepped forward and slipped them from his hand. It quickly disappeared into a pocket of the satin robe.

Alton patted her hip once more. "Same time next week?"

"Uh-huh."

"What are you going to do when they kick everybody out?"

"Move," she whispered.

Tawny opened the door to her apartment.

Alton frowned with concern. "You'll let me know where you move?"

"Of course," she said softly.

When Alton leaned in for a kiss, Tawny steeled herself for his tongue. It was fat and slimy, and he only pushed it in and out, like a meaty jackhammer. After ending his embrace, he stepped into the hallway and never looked back.

Tawny closed the door and repeatedly wiped her tongue across the inside of her hand.

Most of the girls she knew thought they shouldn't have to kiss on the mouth. The movies they watched growing up lied to them. Kissing, like everything, had a price. She didn't do it with everyone, but customers who paid well got special treatment.

As sweaty and fat as the man was, Alton paid handsomely—always tipping her double her requested rate—and he never hurt her. She didn't kiss him the first time. That would have been foolish. It was more than eight months before she let him do it, and he paid for the opportunity.

Tawny grabbed a coffee mug and poured two fingers of Captain Morgan into it. She held the bottle in the air, examining how much was left. She tipped it upside-down and swallowed the final drops that remained. Then she took a big gulp from the cup before setting it in the sink.

On the counter was a yellow notice she had found attached to her front door a week before.

She, along with the other residents, was being evicted from the Hope Apartments. The mass eviction was in preparation for turning the building into condos. Tawny didn't care about the eviction, though. The building was rundown, and she hated her neighbors. Besides, the actual eviction was more than a year away. Why should she care about it today? A lot of things could happen between now and then.

The door to her apartment opened, and Raekwon Gaskin strolled in like he paid for the place—probably because he *did* pay for it. Even though it was hot outside, Tiger wore a hoodie.

"How'd you do with the fat man?"

Tawny pulled the bills from the pocket of her robe and dropped them onto the counter.

Tiger walked over and clutched the money in his fist. Almost immediately, it disappeared inside his pocket.

"Got another regular, or you hitting the stroll?"

She waved a contemptuous hand. "I'm done."

He snatched her by the wrist and yanked her to him. "You're done when I say you're done."

His grip hurt. "I'm tired," she whispered.

"That ass looks like it can take some more mileage."

Tawny jerked her arm free and rubbed her wrist.

"Get to work," he said and turned for the door.

"Tiger," she whispered to stop the man from leaving. She held up the notice. "Another apartment?"

"You got plenty of time." He smirked. "Besides, you need to prove to me that you're worth keeping around."

***

Tawny changed into a red skirt and a black sports bra. The heels she wore hurt her feet, but men wanted to see her like that. She preferred the comfort of tennis shoes, but they dampened business. She was smart enough to give the customers what they wanted.

Before going outside, Tawny rode the elevator up to the sixth floor. She slowly walked down each hallway. Her heels clicked loudly on the linoleum. It was her calling card. There wasn't much money to be had from her neighbors. If one of them came into some quick cash, they often would indulge themselves.

She took the stairs and headed down. On each floor below, she talked with former johns and future hopefuls, but nothing was booked. Once on the street, she turned east and headed along First Avenue.

Her stroll was slow and purposeful but designed to look like a meandering shuffle to an observer. She met the eyes of every man who passed by, whether on foot or in a car.

She took the same route almost every day, although at different times. A trick might be hesitant one day and willing the next. If he couldn't find her, what good would he be?

Tawny stood at the corner of First and Madison and waited to cross the street. A blue Honda Accord pulled up with its passenger side window down.

She bent over to see a middle-aged white man behind the wheel.

"Whisper?" he asked.

Tawny raised an eyebrow.

"My friend recommended you."

Tawny looked up and down the street. "Who?"

"What?"

"Who?" she whispered again.

"Roger."

She knew lots of Rogers. "Which one?"

"Huh?"

Tawny leaned a little closer to the window. "Which one?" she said softly.

The driver glanced around, then said, "Roger Margonis."

Roger was good for recommendations. He'd already referred several clients to her. If he was sending this guy, she shouldn't have to worry. She climbed into the car, and it pulled from the curb.

"Where to?" he asked.

Only regulars got invited to her apartment. "Got a room?"

"You sure talk quiet," he said.

"Got a room?"

"Can we do it in my car?"

Some men liked doing it in their vehicles, but she hated it. She gave him some directions, which he followed, and soon they were parked behind a long vacant office.

"What do you want?" She didn't bother flirting. There was no need to be coy with someone who picked her up—the selling was already over—and the less talking she had to do, the better.

He looked embarrassed when he admitted what he wanted. She named her price, and he never argued. Roger must have told him the rules. He hurriedly pulled some money from his pocket and handed it to her. She tucked the bills into her sports bra as he unbuckled his pants and shoved them to his ankles. He reclined his seat back, and she adjusted her position.

The act went quickly, much faster than she would have expected, but the man was not self-conscious of his performance. Instead, he refastened his pants, repositioned his seat, then turned to her with boyish awe. "Roger was right."

Tawny stared at him.

"Can I see you again?"

She nodded.

"Can we do it in your apartment?"

"No."

"But Roger sees you in your apartment."

"Roger has been with me a long time."

The man seemed to hurt. "So, what? I just need to find you next time?"

She nodded again.

"That's how this works?" There was no malice in his question. He only wanted to know the rules.

"Until we become friends," she said and climbed out of the car.

As the car pulled away, Tawny leaned against the vacant building. She lit a cigarette and inhaled deeply.

***

Tawny walked back to the Hope with a slight detour to the liquor store. She bought a bottle of Captain Morgan Rum and carried it in a brown paper sack.

Once in her apartment, she grabbed a white coffee mug and filled it halfway. She sat at the table and sipped the alcohol. A knock at the door caused her to jump. After setting the cup down, she answered the door, but only by a crack.

A man stood there with a clipboard in his hand. He wore blue jeans and a plaid button-up shirt. His hair was cut short and combed to the side.

Tawny raised an eyebrow.

"Hi, my name is Brendan Miller. I live up on the sixth floor." He pointed upward.

When Tawny didn't answer, Brendan continued.

"Anyway, I'm trying to get everyone's signature on this petition. We're trying to stop the redevelopment of the building."

"Why?" Tawny whispered.

"There's a shortage of low-income housing in our community. I want the city council to protect this building."

Tawny shrugged. "But why?"

Brendan's brow furrowed. "Some of these folks don't have anywhere to go. The council is supporting this redevelopment." He rolled his eyes. "Property rights and all that bull. If we don't fight back soon, many of us will be on the street. A year comes faster than you realize."

A do-gooder, Tawny thought. The easiest thing to do was sign the petition and get him on his way. She took the clipboard and studied the document. It was official, so it would need her real name. She signed it and handed it back.

He read her signature. "Sally Morris. It's nice to meet you." Brendan stuck his hand out, and she shook it. Afterward, he waved the clipboard. "See you later."

Tawny shut the door.

Ten minutes after, she was at the kitchen table with her cup of rum when Tiger walked in the door.

"Break time, I see."

Tawny didn't respond.

"How much have you made?"

She pointed at the table. Tiger walked over and spread the money and coins out with this hand. "Thirty-five dollars and sixty-seven cents? The fuck is this?"

Tawny didn't look at him. Her eyes were focused on her cup.

The tall man walked over and stood directly in front of her. "Where's the rest?"

"That's it."

Tiger smacked the cup from her hand. It crashed onto the floor and spilled its remaining contents on the already stained carpet.

"Are you holding out?"

She shook her head.

"You're holding out."

"No!" she shouted. Her voice was raspy and deep.

Tiger sneered. "I hate the way you sound."

Tawny lowered her eyes.

The pimp snatched the bills from the table. Then he swiped the coins across the table, flinging them across the apartment. "Double your efforts, or I'll double the punishment."

Tawny didn't make eye contact with the tall man.

"More ass equals more green. It ain't rocket science. That's whore math. Understand?"

He walked out of the apartment, slamming the door behind him.

***

The following morning, Tawny woke early. After another cup of Captain Morgan, she threw the empty bottle away and took a shower.

She'd just finished slipping into a pair of jeans and a T-shirt when there was a knock on the door. She opened it and was greeted by Brendan Miller.

"Hi, Sally." His grin was wide and stupid—only citizens smiled that big. "Want to grab some coffee?"

Tawny cocked her head. Why was a citizen living at the Hope?

"You drink coffee, don't you?"

Tawny nodded once.

"Because if you don't, we could go get something instead—tea or a soda, maybe."

She didn't want to start working yet. There was plenty of time for that.

"Coffee," she whispered and held up a finger for him to wait.

She grabbed her oversized purse and stepped into the hallway. After locking the door, she turned to Brendan and nodded.

***

They were seated at the Rocket Bakery at Cedar and First. The trendy coffee shop was packed.

"Busy," Tawny whispered.

"It's Saturday."

Tawny nodded. Days of the week had little impact on her.

Brendan sipped his coffee and studied her. Tawny had ordered an iced latte and now pushed the concoction around with her straw.

"You don't say much, do you?"

She shrugged.

"Do you mind if I ask how old you are?"

"Twenty-seven," she whispered. "You?"

"Twenty-five."

She asked softly, "What do you do?"

"Spot work, mostly. You know, for Labor Ready. Ever hear of that?"

She nodded.

"I'm also taking a couple night classes at the community college."

"For?"

"English and math, but they're pre-reqs. I'm going for my AA in business. When I get that, I'll transfer to Eastern."

"Huh."

"I didn't go to college after high school," Brendan said. "I wanted to see the country, so I hitchhiked around until I ended up here."

"Where are you from?" she whispered.

"Mankato. Minnesota. Ever hear of it?"

She shook her head.

"I drifted down to Florida for a bit, then over to Texas, up through Nevada. I liked Nevada—that was pretty cool, except for the summer." He waited for her to say something, but when she didn't, he continued. "That was supposed to be a joke. I guess it wasn't a good one, though. Ever been to Vegas?"

She again shook her head.

"When I made it here, I sort of lost the will to go any further. It feels like this is where I'm supposed to be. Like this is home, you know?"

Spokane was the only home she'd ever known. If she could figure a way from it, she would run and never look back. She hated this town. Tawny stopped moving her straw up and down in her cup. She whispered, "Why do you live at the Hope?"

"What do you mean?"

"You're smart."

Brendan blushed. "I'm not smart."

"Sure."

"If I was smart, I wouldn't be in rehab. I wouldn't have been arrested, and I wouldn't be on probation."

Tawny put her elbow on the table and rested her chin in her hand. So, he wasn't a citizen, she thought.

"You want to know why I was arrested."

She nodded.

"You can't move about the country without money."

She hadn't thought of that.

"Before I left Minnesota, both my parents were dead, and my brother was in jail. I figured nothing was keeping me there anymore, so I might as well go someplace warm. Unfortunately, I didn't have any money, so I started breaking into homes. Everywhere I went, it felt the same— depressing and lonely. My perception of the world was all messed up because I was using pretty heavy."

Tawny frowned.

"Oxy."

She cocked her head. She knew a lot of people who used that drug. It did terrible things to them.

"What I didn't realize," Brendan continued, "is I kept running from town to town, trying to escape the thing I could never escape."

She watched him, waiting for him to tell her what that inescapable thing was.

"Me," he said, tapping his chest. "It wasn't until I made it here that I was arrested and ended up in a rehab program. That's when I realized I had the opportunity to do something with my life, but it was up to me to make the most of it. So, I ended up at the Hope, which I think is pretty ironic. What a name for that place."

They were silent for a moment, both sipping their coffees. Finally, Brendan spoke. "Why do you live there?"

Tawny's brow crinkled, but she didn't answer his question.

"A pretty girl like you shouldn't be there."

"Do you know what I do?"

Brendan leaned in to hear her better.

"I'm a working girl," she whispered, softer than usual. It was the politest way she knew how to describe what she did.

"We all have to work."

"Not that kind of work."

"Oh."

There was nothing more to say than that.

They sat quietly for a few moments. She fiddled with her coffee mug, and Brendan watched the cars passing on First Avenue. When he eventually faced her again, he asked, "Have you ever had a boyfriend? Like a real one?"

She bowed her head. She hadn't.

***

Together, Tawny and Brendan walked back to the apartment building. After she revealed her occupation, much of their time had been spent in awkward silence.

At the door to her apartment, she softly said, "Thank you."

"Why do you whisper?" His words were non-threatening and non-judgmental.

She thought about telling him of the attack she suffered. How the man wrapped his large hands around her throat and tried to choke her to death. How she survived the attack, but her voice did not. How the doctor said the fractures in her laryngeal cartilage never healed correctly, meaning her dream of someday singing would remain unrealized. She thought about telling him all those things but instead said, "It's not important."

Tawny entered her apartment but turned to see Brendan watching her expectantly. She didn't know what he waited for, and she didn't want to ask, only to be disappointed.

She slowly closed the door.

***

The coffee with Brendan had been nice. She hadn't had a conversation with a man who wasn't looking to buy her, rescue her, or hurt her in a long time. All the men in her life now were pimps, johns, cops, or social workers.

Brendan had been a pleasant diversion but drinking coffee with him wasn't going to make Tiger happy.

She needed to work.

***

Tiger showed up at eight. His walk was unsure, and his lips were twisted into a crooked smile.

"Got something to drink?"

Tawny pointed to a newly opened bottle of Captain Morgan on the kitchen counter. Tiger pulled open a couple of cabinet doors before he found another white coffee cup like the one she held.

He filled his and walked over to the couch. He sat next to her and put his arm around her shoulders.

"Hi, baby," he cooed. "How we doin'?"

"Fine." She set her cup on the end table and steeled herself for what was coming.

When she first hooked up with Tiger, she bought into his stories. She believed he loved her and would take care of her. She believed this would only be part-time, that she was better than his other girls. She thought the two of them would run away and start a new life. She also believed he was genuinely sorry the first time he hit her and that he would never do it again.

Over time, those dreams faded like her childhood fantasies of being a famous singer.

Tawny now knew she was tainted goods. Her voice was gone, her looks were fading, and most men would never accept a whore, even a former one, as a wife. Tiger preached that to her and the other girls regularly.

But this night wouldn't be a beat-down, either verbal or physical. It was merely her turn to take care of his needs.

He said things to her that he thought she would like but which she simply ignored. She'd worked hard today. She'd been with several men before calling it, and now Tiger wanted his turn.

She reached over and grabbed her coffee cup. With a large swallow, she finished off the rum.

Still ignoring the sugary words he whispered, she reached over and unzipped Tiger's pants. The sooner she got it over with, the sooner she could go to sleep.

***

The following day, Brendan knocked on her door.

Tawny's eyes widened upon seeing him with two cups of coffee in a cardboard tray and a small paper bag.

He lifted both items. "I thought I'd surprise you. I brought croissants."

She frantically shook her head. "I can't."

Brendan lowered his arms. "Did I go too far?"

"I can't," she repeated.

"Okay. Want to meet later and go to the park? It's a beautiful morning."

"No."

She started to close the door, but a hand wrapped around it. Tawny stiffened.

"He doesn't look like he pays," Tiger said.

Tawny looked back to see the tall man in only his boxers. When she faced Brendan, he stared straight ahead.

"Looks like you got a man on the side, Whisper. Is that true?"

Tawny shook her head.

"Does he *want* to be your man? Maybe take you away?"

Neither Tawny nor Brendan moved. Tiger stepped around Tawny and took the coffee and paper bag from Brendan. He handed them to Tawny.

Tiger stood five inches taller and almost fifty pounds heavier than Brendan.

The smaller man thrust his chin out and defiantly said, "Sally doesn't belong to you."

"*Sally?*" Tiger eyed Tawny. "You told him your birth name?"

"I—" Tawny began to protest, but Tiger spun quickly back to Brendan.

"She belongs to me. You can rent her, but I *own* her."

"Nobody owns her."

Tiger grabbed Brendan by the throat and pinned him against the far wall of the hallway. Brendan held helplessly onto the tall man's wrist.

"I will always own her! She is mine—bought and paid for—many times over."

"No!" Brendan rasped as he tried to pry the man's hands from his throat.

Tiger punched Brendan in the stomach, doubling the smaller man over and dropping him to the floor. "Stay away."

Tawny stood still the entire time the assault occurred. The paper sack and coffees were in her hands as tears filled her eyes.

"Get back in there." Tiger pointed into her apartment. "You and me got some talking to do." Fury burned in his eyes. "Seems you forget the rules to this game."

***

Tawny walked the sixth-floor hallway, her heels clicking loudly. As she passed an apartment with a missing number, its door opened, and Brendan stuck his head out. "Hi, Sally."

"I can't," she whispered.

"You can't, what? You can't say 'hi'?" Brendan stepped outside his apartment. "Are you that scared?"

"He loves me." Tawny didn't believe the lie.

"He loves you? He makes you have sex with other men for money. That's what love is?"

Tawny's face warmed, and she walked away.

He trotted up next to her, his bare feet slapping the linoleum of the hallway's floor. "I'm sorry."

She stopped but didn't look at him.

Brendan reached out and lightly touched her arm. "Listen, I *really* am sorry. I'm a jerk. If you want to be with him, that's okay if that's what you want. But if you're with him because you're afraid, then break free and be with me."

"I can't." She hurried to the stairwell. She wanted to get off this floor.

***

That night, Brendan showed up at Tawny's apartment. She didn't want to let him in, but he was insistent.

"I've got a plan." He closed the door behind him.

Tawny set her mugful of Captain Morgan on the table. "Plan?"

"You can never be free of Tiger as long as he's your pimp."

Tawny crossed her arms. "You want to take his place?"

Brendan stood in front of Tawny. "That's crazy. I want to be your boyfriend."

She touched the side of his face. "This isn't a movie."

"What are you talking about?"

"This," she pointed to herself, "is an illusion. I'm a lie. You don't want me."

"Don't say that. I'll work out a deal with him. We can come to some agreement."

"Tiger doesn't negotiate."

Brendan smiled. "Everyone negotiates."

"Not him."

"I'll make it so he has to let you go."

"He won't," she whispered.

Brendan lifted the front of his shirt. Poking out from the waistband was the butt of a gun.

She covered her mouth with a hand. "Where did you get that?"

"It doesn't matter. I'll make him see."

"No!" Tawny said. This time, her voice was loud and raspy. "He'll hurt you! You can't beat him."

"Your voice. What's wrong?"

Tawny returned to the kitchen table to retrieve her cup. After a sip, she whispered, "Damage to my throat. Another reason to stay away."

"Did he do that?"

"No, and it's old news. Leave him alone. It's not worth it."

"Run away with me." Brendan dropped to his knees and grabbed her hand. "Please."

"Where would we go? You've got no money. I'd be on the street in a week to support us."

Brendan shook his head. "I wouldn't let that happen. I'd do construction. You could be a waitress."

She wrinkled her nose. "A waitress? Me?"

"We can make it work. I promise."

The door to the apartment swung open, and Tiger stepped in. He froze when he saw Brendan kneeling in front of Tawny. "The fuck?"

Tawny jumped around Brendan and ran to Tiger. She held her hands up in a calming manner. "It's not what you think."

Tiger shoved her to the side. "It's exactly what it looks like."

Brendan stood with his feet wide and his hands balled. "We're leaving."

"Leaving?"

"That's right. Sally is coming with me."

"Whisper ain't goin' nowhere."

Brendan tugged the gun free from his waistband. He pointed it at the bigger man. "We're leaving."

"Don't," Tawny said, her voice low and husky.

"You goin' shoot me?" Tiger asked. "With that itty-bitty twenty-two?"

"I don't want to."

"It won't be the first time I been shot."

The gun shook in Brendan's hands.

"Did you go to the store and pick out that girl gun?"

Tiger stepped forward towards Brendan.

"Stop moving!" Brendan yelled.

Tawny covered her face with her hands and screamed. It was loud and ugly.

Tiger took another step and was within arm's reach of Brendan.

"Listen, kid. She's no good. You're ruining your life over nothing."

"No," Brendan said. "She's—"

Tiger's hand whipped out and smacked the gun to the side. It fired once before the pimp grabbed the smaller man. He overpowered Brendan as both men now struggled for control of the weapon. Another round fired, and Brendan crumpled to the floor. A bullet had entered under his chin, and he was now bleeding on the carpet.

Tiger stepped back from the dead man, and Tawny continued her croaky scream.

The pimp stepped over to her and slapped the hands covering her face. "Whisper!"

She stopped screaming but kept her hands over her face.

"Get yourself under control."

Tawny peered between her fingers.

"The cops will be here soon, and you're gonna have to explain this."

She lowered her hands and looked at the body on the floor. She quickly averted her eyes.

"Get it together."

"I'm telling them the truth."

The pimp smirked. "The truth?" He pointed at Brendan. "The truth is that man wouldn't be dead except for you. You filled his head with thoughts. You should have set him straight. Instead, you let him believe things he shouldn't have been believing."

Tears ran down Tawny's face.

"That boy shot himself. My hand wasn't even on the gun. And if you try to jam me up, I swear I'll make you hurt like you've never hurt before. You know I can do that, too, don't you?"

She continued to cry.

"Tell me, you know I can hurt you."

"You can hurt me," she whispered.

The tall man put his hand on the side of her head and rubbed her hair. He leaned in and stared into her eyes. "But I would never hurt you, Sally. You're a good girl." He kissed the side of her cheek. "My best girl."

He softly patted her hip, then walked out, making sure to wipe the doorknob as he did so.

Tawny stood in her apartment, crying. She turned and stared at the body lying on the floor. It jerked once, a final spasm perhaps, but it scared her nonetheless.

She screamed a low, grating howl filled with terror and frustration.

When she calmed herself, she poured some rum into a mug and sat. She only had a few minutes to come up with a story before the cops arrived.

She'd blame everything on Brendan, of course. She would tell them he was a love-struck customer who killed himself because she wouldn't run away with him. Yeah, that would be the story. It was unforgettable and straightforward.

Tawny swallowed the rest of the rum in her cup.

Besides, it was the story she wanted to believe.

Angel

I've heard she's beautiful.
I've never seen her, but that's what they've said.
Born out of pain and fear, she stands without modesty or embarrassment.
Long, black hair flows over softly rounded shoulders.
A hip juts forward in mocking promise.
Her beauty is unparalleled.
At least, that's what they've said.

***

Amidst his horrible screams and my terrified shrieks, I struggled to break free from his grasp. Even if I managed to get loose, there was nowhere to go. We were caged animals, and nature had dictated him the predator. There was no illusion as to what that made me.

He let go of my neck and punched me in the stomach. I dropped to my knees.

"Piece of shit," he shouted before striking me on the side of the head. "This cell is mine!"

I fell forward to my hands and coughed blood.

He hollered, "Everything in here is mine!"

Stepping to the side, he kicked my ribs. I collapsed to the floor, covered my head with my hands, and desperately sucked for air. The pain in my chest scared me as much as his words.

Facedown on the concrete, I didn't see him move behind me. He booted me in the groin, and I vomited.

"Don't puke on my floor!"

I gasped for oxygen through a puddle of my own sick, the smell of which burned my nostrils.

He grabbed my hair and yanked my head back. His hot breath was in my ear.

"Everything belongs to me. Understand? That includes you."

Bile rose in my throat.

"Don't ever tell me *no* again."

I blacked out when he slammed my head against the floor.

***

Her eyes have seen your sins.
They will haunt your dreams but warm you in the cold.
They beg for your love.
But it's the eyes that break your heart.
I have painted an image of her in my mind from their descriptions.
Sometimes, I believe she is lovely.
Most of the time, I wish I could kill her.

***

I've killed before.

She was the woman I loved.

It's not as hard as people imagine.

In my old life, I saw murderers on television and wondered how they could kill someone. I could never understand the lack of empathy it took to end the life of another human being.

Now, I fully understand.

When she told me she wanted a divorce, I wrapped my hands around Lorraine's throat. She taunted that she would take the kids, the house, and everything I worked for. She knew about the babysitter's abortion and promised to tell everyone. She laughed when she said she would ruin my life.

I couldn't have that. I had worked too hard and for too long to let her rip everything away. As I choked her, she dug her manicured nails into my face. When it was done, I stood over her. It had been surprisingly easy.

That's when I cried.

***

Delicate wings extend from her back.
Some describe the wings as being golden, while others say they are like clouds.
No one disagrees with their beauty, though.
But they all say the wings can't compare to the eyes that stare at you knowingly.

***

I pled guilty to Second Degree Murder, and the judge sentenced me to twenty years. The Old Testament demands an eye for an eye, but I killed my wife and got twenty years. I don't think the judge really cared how long I went away. Instead, he consulted a little card before determining the amount of time he handed out.

While in the courtroom, my attorney whispered into my ear that if I could avoid trouble, I'd be out in twelve years. That sounded good at the time, but even twelve minutes with Elroy Samuel Hawkins was too long.

The Hammer is my cellmate. He's six feet two, two hundred and fifty pounds of muscle and hate. He shaves his head bald every morning, but you can see his brown hair is receding if you look closely enough. With his permanent scowl, everyone gives Hawkins a wide berth.

They call him the Hammer because he bludgeoned two families to death with a wooden-handled tool of the same name. He slipped into the first house and killed an elderly couple, along with their visiting grandson. The second family of victims was a young couple and their three daughters. He was shot when he broke into the third house, which happened to be owned by a city police officer.

By the time Hawkins made it to the hospital, he was in critical condition. The staff worked for hours to save Elroy's life. When they walked away from the operating table, Hawkins lay in critical but stable condition, with the rest of his life still in front of him. Unfortunately, there were eight bodies in the morgue the Hammer had to answer for.

He agreed to a guilty plea for life in prison.

The prosecuting attorney made a big show of how his office saved the city the expense of a trial that would surely have been a media fiasco. Nothing drives ratings like the horror of a murder spree on the evening news.

In protecting their decision not to go to trial, the attorneys also argued the death penalty wasn't guaranteed even with a guilty conviction. The final point in defending their position was Hawkins's plea protected the city against the murderer being ruled insane and avoiding prison all together by way of a mental institution.

Hawkins *was* insane, though.

He'd been raised in the system of orphanages, foster homes, juvenile detention, and finally prison. He'd been out of jail for a total of three weeks before his killing spree with the hammer. Hawkins needed to get back to prison where he had power, where he was respected and understood the rules. It hardly seemed fair that someone like me—someone who'd never thought about murder until that fateful moment—should have to share a cell with that tower of evil.

Three days after the first beating he gave me, Hawkins forced my head into a pillow with his massive hand. Two members of his crew held me as Hawkins pulled my pants down.

"Baby," he growled, "now you're gonna find out why they really call me the Hammer."

I screamed as he pushed inside. His cronies laughed wildly.

One of them asked if he could take a turn when he was done.

Between grunts, Hawkins growled, "This one is mine, and I ain't sharin'. Virgin pussy is hard to find."

***

The woman wasn't born of love.
The beauty that brings hope to others sprang from the evil minds of men.
Only one wicked man knows her perfect curves through his touch.
I've touched her in the dark but can't distinguish her beauty.

***

Prison is harsh for good men who, but for a moment, only committed a single crime. Men whose number one priority in life was seeking the comfort of status and wealth. Men like that, men like me, are chum for the prison system. Wherever the prison, the moment we walk in, we're sheep thrown into a lion's pride.

When the needle first pricked my skin, I jumped, but the hands held me down. I'd never felt it before. They say some get addicted to the sensation, but I hated it. I wanted to scream, but Hawkins had stuffed his sweaty T-shirt in my mouth.

He leaned over me so I could see his face. "You move again and screw up the line, I'll beat your ass."

Hawkins had brought the Marvel to our cell to ink me.

They called him the Marvel because of his artwork and the Spider-man tattoo he wore on his back. In the real world, the Marvel had earned his living as a tattoo artist. That was before he fell in love with meth. Once he picked up his second strike for manufacturing, the system sent him here, where the general population soon discovered his talents.

When the cronies finally let me stand, the Marvel had already packed up and left the cell. Hawkins smiled at the new artwork that adorned the chest above my heart.

An evil smile spread across Hawkins's face. "You ruin that tat by doing something stupid, and I'll hurt you. Bad. You'll wish you never met me."

I stepped over to the wall and gazed into the small, round mirror. I saw the reflection and started to cry.

Hawkins came up behind me and rubbed my shoulders as the tears left tracks down my face.

"It's beautiful, isn't it?" His raspy voice crawled into my ears and sent shivers through my body.

On my chest, about three inches in length, shone the fresh ink of a hammer. I closed my eyes from the sight.

I felt Hawkins's lips on my neck. "It's so beautiful."

***

Her skin is white like mine. I am sure of that much.
It's free of blemishes.
She has no moles, no scars, and no freckles.
She is pure.
Even though she has known no sin, evil adores her beauty and longs for just a glance at her perfection.

***

Two Hispanic inmates attacked me in the shower.

It was the one hundred and seventy-sixth day of my sentence. The two—a small, portly guy with pocked skin and his skeleton-like partner—surrounded me. I had just finished shampooing my hair, the white foam still dripping down to my chest.

"Where's your precious Hammer, *ese*?" the fat one asked from behind.

I braced myself for a fight. "I don't know and don't care."

"Trouble in paradise?" The skinny one asked as he continued to wash his genitals.

"Shut up."

My head snapped back as the fat one pushed me. I fell to the floor and skidded across the wet concrete. The portly bastard cracked a joke about dropping the soap.

The skinny one stroked his manhood and grinned. "Been a while since I had some white ass."

When I felt the fat one grab at my waist, I fought back. I rolled over and kicked upward into his testicles. He screamed and clutched his groin. I scrambled to my feet and turned to face the skinny one.

He charged me, and his cock bounced wildly. I threw a punch, but he slipped under it and hit me in the side of my stomach. I fell to the floor, hugging my side.

The skinny one hit me a couple of more times before I sprawled onto the cement shower room floor. They stood over me, smiling.

"The meat's always sweeter when they fight," the skinny one said.

The fat one got down on his knees and touched his limp penis to my lips. "Suck this hard. If you don't, your life won't be worth shit."

Afraid to fight back anymore, I opened my mouth.

The skinny one moved behind me.

"Double-teaming a white boy." The skeleton giggled as he tried to push into me.

When I heard a new set of footsteps enter the shower room, the warm embrace of darkness worked its way over me. Before I passed out, I saw the Hammer walking with a mop handle clenched in his fist.

I realized with terror just what the two families saw when he was in their homes.

***

***

Several weeks passed before Hawkins was brought back to our cell.

While he spent the time in solitary, I relished the destruction he brought to the Hispanics. He beat them both with the mop handle and his fists.

The fat one suffered a broken elbow and cheekbone. The skinny one wasn't as lucky. He lost an eye, most of his teeth and ended up with the mop handle in his rectum. By the time the medics arrived to help me, blood was everywhere in the shower room. Some of it was mine, but not much.

My satisfaction in his revenge was replaced with the realization of why he did it.

"You know you owe me, right?" Hawkins asked when he sat next to me on my bunk. The springs moaned under his weight.

I nodded with the awareness that the repayment of my sins had only just begun.

"I know how you can make it up to me. I thought about it non-stop while in the hole. It kept me going."

The needle prick on my lower back was familiar but unwanted. However, I didn't hate it this time—doing so would be worthless.

Instead, I tried to picture the lake cabin I once owned and the way the sun shone off the water. We spent a couple of peaceful summers there as a young family. The image glowed with intensity in my mind.

I prayed for God to wake me from my nightmare and place me there. He ignored my plea.

During the initial inking, my knees were on the concrete while I laid chest down on my bunk. We had to stop several times so I could get up and let the blood return to my lower legs. Whenever there was a break, I would walk to the corner of our cell and just lean into it, my head pressed against the concrete walls.

After the first session, the Marvel let me stand while he finished the filling in and touch-up.

The whole process took several weeks to complete. I never spoke during any of it. I would just take it quietly and clean up the bloody clothes the Marvel used. Every time Marvel finished a different portion of the tattoo, Hawkins beamed with pride and excitement.

With the process complete, the Marvel left the cell after receiving some words of praise from Hawkins and his friends. The Hammer told them all to go, then came over to me as I leaned into the corner.

"It's beautiful." His raspy voice filled me with dread.

"I'm sure it is," I fought to keep the tears back.

"She's beautiful. Wanna see? We could grab the mirror and go to the shower so you can check her out."

"I don't want to see it." Bile rose in my throat.

"Why not?" His voice had turned hard.

Picking my words carefully, I said, "Because it's yours. She's for you."

The Hammer stepped behind me and slid his hand around to my bare stomach. "You've made me very happy."

"I owed you."

"Come here." He guided me away from the corner. He then pushed me down onto the bunk and pulled my underwear down.

"She's beautiful. She's an angel."

I ground my teeth as he pushed inside. The thought of spending twenty years in Hawkins's cell overwhelmed me, and my stomach burned.

"You're my angel," he said after an excited grunt. His fingers carefully outlined the tattoo on my lower back while keeping his left hand on my hip. "You are such a beautiful woman."

My fists clenched the blanket on my bunk as his rhythm increased. His voice and breathing were excited as he made love to the heavenly vision the Marvel had created.

"I love you, Angel," he moaned.

I bit the inside of my cheek to stop from crying.

Inheritance of the Meek

Gabriel Forsberg shifted uncomfortably in the booth. Next to him, Harvey Mott sat too close, and the man smelled more pungent than usual. Harv always had a working man's musk, but today he desperately needed a bath.

Across the table, their employer watched Harv. Maurice Shelley wasn't the kind to pretend not to notice a smell. When Maurice's gaze dropped to his hands, Gabe scooted further into the corner of the booth.

"It's a simple job," Maurice said. "Just find out what he told the cops."

"Yeah," Harv agreed. "Simple."

Gabe surreptitiously watched his partner. Harv's eyes were slitted, and his fingers drummed an antsy rhythm on the edge of their booth.

Maurice dropped a large manila envelope onto the table. Harv didn't reach for it, and Gabe knew better than to try.

Their employer was a tall, thin man with thick, black-rimmed glasses. His curly hair was gray and thinning. Gabe thought he might look funny if it weren't for the crazy look in the man's eyes. It seemed to suggest Maurice would just as soon slit Gabe's throat as meet him for this lunch.

The sun beamed in through the windows and gave the little restaurant a hazy feel. The diner seemed slow for midday, but Gabe guessed that's how most things were in Metaline Falls. The town was on Highway 31, one hundred ten miles north of Spokane and roughly twenty minutes south of the Canadian border.

"He's ten miles from here," Maurice said, "in a cabin owned by his father-in-law."

In a low voice, but with quick words, Harv said, "What did he do?" His fingers now jumped along the edge of the table.

Maurice leaned back against the booth. "You okay?"

Harv's drumming stopped, and he glanced at Gabe, then back to their employer. "I'm doing great. Why?"

"You don't look so great."

Harv turned away to watch the other patrons in the restaurant. "I'm doing fine, Mo. Right as rain. You don't have to worry about me."

Gabe wouldn't have the guts to call their employer by a nickname, but Harv and Maurice had worked together for years. It wasn't the first time Gabe heard his partner do it, but it was the first time Harv ever did it at the beginning of a job.

"If you say so, Harvey."

Gabe let out the breath he didn't realize he'd been holding.

"So, this guy," Harv said, "he knows you're looking for him? That's why he's up here."

"He's scared. He can't take back what he did, and we sure as hell aren't going to let him. Sooner or later, we were going to find out."

"We always do," Harv said.

Maurice raised his eyebrows. "We?"

"You. I was using *we* as in the collective."

"This isn't Russia, Harvey. There isn't any fucking collective here." Maurice tapped his chest. "I found him."

Harv looked at Gabe, then back to their employer. "You found him, Mo. I totally get that."

Maurice shifted in his seat. "This time of the year, Allen usually takes a vacation up to the cabin. I guess he's trying to keep things normal for his family."

"His family?" Gabe asked.

Their employer tsked. "Wife and daughter."

Harv glowered at Gabe before asking, "Any restrictions on them?"

Maurice's eyelids drooped. "If he admits to what he did, let them be, but if he refuses—" He dragged a thumb across his throat.

The waitress approached the table with the men's order. She was an older woman with big hips, rounded shoulders, and a puffy face. She didn't make small talk as she set the plates in front of them. They didn't bother to coax any chatter from her.

When she left, Gabe asked, "What are their names?"

Maurice sipped his iced tea before saying, "Why's it matter, Gabriel?"

Harv glared at him.

"In case—"

"In case, what?" Maurice said.

"Well, if we need to ask them where Allen is. If he's not there when we show up, I mean. Knowing a name would go a long way in playing nice."

Their employer inhaled deeply and seemed to consider Gabe's words. "The wife is Sylvia. The daughter is Taylor."

Harv leaned in. "Any cops with him?"

Maurice shrugged. "How would I know? Do your homework."

Harvey thought for a moment, then nodded. Gabe nodded, too, and felt like a dumbass for doing so.

"Who is he?" Harv asked.

Maurice tapped a single finger on the envelope, then pushed it between Harvey and Gabriel. "He's an accountant. Handled some investments for us." Maurice spun his plate to examine his entrée. "When will they ever learn? These guys continue to hire these Jew—" Maurice eyed Gabe. He didn't apologize, but he nodded. It was the closest Gabe would get to hearing an apology from his employer.

Maurice continued. "They hire these outsiders to watch our money, yet they're always the first to rat." He picked up his fork and cut a piece of meatloaf. He shoved it in his mouth and started to say something but stopped. A grin appeared while he chewed and revealed bits of food pasted on his teeth. After he swallowed, Maurice pointed his fork at the plate. "That's good."

Harv didn't say anything. Instead, his fingers returned to tapping out the antsy rhythm along the booth.

When Gabe noticed Maurice eyeing him, he figured the employer was waiting for him to acknowledge his review. Gabe picked up his fork, cut a piece of the meatloaf on his own plate, and shoved it into his mouth. It could have tasted like garbage, and Gabe still would have happily agreed with Maurice's assessment. If they were going to take the job, and it looked like they were, it didn't make sense to piss off the man.

The meatloaf was tasteless, but Gabe mimicked Maurice's smile and chewed as if his life depended on it.

The employer shoved another bite in his mouth and continued talking. "Directions are in the envelope. You'll get paid when you're done."

Harv ran his fingers through his long black hair, then snatched the envelope. "Have it ready," he said. Then he slid out of the booth and headed toward the door.

Maurice cut into his meatloaf again, but no longer cared if anyone liked it as much as he did.

Gabe took the hint and went after Harv.

***

They'd been driving north for only two minutes when Harv told Gabe to pull into a gas station at the edge of town.

"We got a full tank," Gabe said.

"I said pull over."

Gabe shrugged, spun the wheel, and bounced into the parking lot.

"Wait here." Harv didn't bother closing his door. He entered the building but reappeared almost immediately. He then walked around the corner and disappeared.

Gabe flipped on the radio and searched for some music. Most of the Spokane stations reach as far up as Metaline Falls. The ones that did played country music, which he hated, or had some idiots blathering on about politics—he hated that even more.

When Harv climbed back in, he angrily turned off the radio. "Let's go." He slammed his door closed.

"What was that about?"

Harv had a wild look in his eyes. "You asking about my bowel movements?"

"No."

"Then shut up and drive."

Gabe did just that.

***

The Pend Oreille River runs along Highway 31 for a bit but, eventually, the road moves away. Their car—a dark green Chevy Impala—handled like a dream. It should. It was clean with appropriate papers, which meant it wasn't stolen.

Gabe turned the radio on again and searched for a station. Without looking at Harv, he said, "We're not gonna hurt the wife and kid, right?"

"Huh?"

Gabe turned down the stereo and repeated his question.

Harv stared at him so long that Gabe turned the stereo back up. Harv snapped it off.

"Do I have to worry about you?"

Gabe's safest response was to keep his mouth closed. He didn't need to be reminded of how he screwed up their last job. Harv made a clicking sound with his teeth, pulled out his gun, and removed the magazine. Gabe wasn't sure why his partner did that. They'd just cleaned their guns and loaded them in Spokane. Removing the magazine seemed like something a civilian would do.

Using the directions from the envelope, Gabe turned on Slate Creek Road and found the house without much hassle. He slowed the car, and Harv reinserted the magazine into his gun. His partner pulled slightly back on the slide to ensure a bullet was in the chamber. Again, this was something they'd already done in Spokane.

They went slowly by the house. It was a two-story cabin, bigger than any house Gabe had ever lived in. A burgundy Lexus was parked in front.

There was a long entry road to the home. A patch of forest was its backyard, and the Pend Oreille River ran behind the trees. Anyone approaching in daylight would easily be seen.

"No cop cars," Harv said.

"Maybe they parked around back."

"Turn around."

Taking his eyes off the road to watch Harv, Gabe asked, "Why?"

"We can take care of this now. Why waste an opportunity for quick money?"

"In broad daylight?"

Harv eyed Gabe, and a sneer formed. It slowly faded until he sucked in his lips and nodded. "You're right. Good call."

Gabe looked ahead again as he continued to drive. Something wasn't right. That wasn't like Harv. He knew better than to make a play now, and he sure as hell would never tell Gabe he was right if he'd been called out on a mistake.

"Let's find a back way in," Harv said.

"Along the river?"

"That'll work. I just don't want to wait."

"It would be better at night."

Harv shook his head. "Fuck that noise. Bears and shit could be in those woods. If there's something in there, I'd rather see them in the daylight. Besides, I don't want you slipping in the river. I know you can't swim."

Gabe challenged his partner once. He knew better than to try it again.

The first chance he had, Gabe pulled the car onto a forest road and hid it in a clump of trees.

***

Harv didn't bother concealing his movements through the patch of forest. The river made some noise, but it didn't drown out their ruckus. They moved so quickly that the crunching leaves, small tree branches breaking, and heavy breathing would alert a deaf man to their approach. If Harv feared bears or other wild animals, he wasn't acting like it.

The smell of pine trees and dirt was overwhelming. Sweat rolled down Gabe's forehead and stung his eyes.

"Slow down," Gabe said, partly to reduce their racket, but mainly to catch his breath. He carried a shotgun and a backpack with the rest of their gear. His gun, a Smith & Wesson revolver, was tucked into his jeans and pressed against the small of his back.

Harv glanced over his shoulder as the gun in his hand dangled by his side. "Let's go."

"You're too noisy," Gabe whispered, "and we've gotta be getting close to the house by now."

His partner paused and looked around. "Yeah," he said with a slow nod. "You're probably right. Good call."

There Harv went again, giving credit for an idea that wasn't his. It was unsettling to Gabe.

They continued walking, but at a more measured pace now. Gabe fell in behind his partner, struggling to control not only his breathing but also the thoughts about Harvey now running through his head.

***

They stopped in the woods, directly behind the house they saw earlier. The river was at their backs.

Leaning on a tree for support, Gabe asked, "What's the plan?"

"Go in fast," Harv said. "There should only be Allen, his wife, and daughter."

"Who gets who?"

Harv shook his head as if he were disappointed in Gabe's question. "We've done this before."

"What if there's a cop?"

"You going pussy on me?"

"No." Harv's recklessness made Gabe nervous, but he couldn't admit it out loud. They didn't have that kind of relationship.

"Then let's go."

Harv didn't wait for Gabe to protest further and stepped out of the woods. He hurried to the back of the house. When he made it, Gabe left the safety of the forest and ran.

Next to the back door was a red can of gas. A weed-eater lay on the ground nearby.

Harv opened the door and was inside quickly with his gun clutched in his right hand. Catching the screen door before it could bang shut, Gabe followed behind him. He brought the butt of the shotgun up to his shoulder. He should have been in the lead, but Harv wasn't waiting for him—they were doing it all wrong.

They moved through the kitchen into a large living room that made up half the house's first level. In the far corner, a dark-haired man wearing khakis and a polo shirt reclined on the sofa. His head was back, his feet were up on a coffee table, and he snored loudly. A holstered gun lay on the couch next to him.

Harv stopped and leveled his gun at the man. Then he pointed up the stairs.

Gabe didn't move. His eyes were riveted to the cop. Harv angrily waved his hand and again pointed up the stairs.

Embarrassed for staring at the lawman, Gabe nodded. He quietly climbed the steps.

The first room, a large bedroom, was empty. The bed hadn't been made. Along the wall were two open suitcases on the floor. Clothes spilled out of them both.

A bathroom was next. It, too, was empty.

From the next room, murmuring voices came—they seemed light and happy. A girl giggled. Gabe moved to the door, which had been left slightly open. Through the crack of the door, he could see Allen Jefferson, his wife, Sylvia, and their daughter, Taylor. The kid looked about six years old.

The family was sitting on the floor, playing a game. Sylvia leaned against a full-sized bed.

Allen rolled the dice and moved his piece several spots before his daughter thrust out her hand and announced, "That's my railroad. Two hundred dollars."

Using the barrel of the shotgun, Gabe pushed the door slowly open. Allen and Taylor didn't see him, but Sylvia did. Her eyes widened, and she screamed.

Downstairs, a single gunshot fired.

Allen stood and spun to face Gabe. Sylvia grabbed her daughter and clutched her.

"What do you want?" Allen asked.

"Quiet," Gabe said.

Taylor cried and held her mother. Sylvia did her best to calm her.

Heavy footsteps moved quickly around the ground floor. It was only a couple of seconds later when Harv yelled, "Clear."

"Clear," Gabe called back. To Allen, he asked, "Got a cell phone?"

"No."

Gabe lifted the shotgun. "Empty your pockets."

Reluctantly, the man reached into his front pockets and pulled out a set of keys and a lighter. He dropped them to the floor.

"Let me see the back."

The husband slowly turned around with his hands at his side. His red and black bowling shirt hung below his waist.

"Lift your shirt."

Allen did as he was told. There were objects in both back pockets.

"Empty them."

The husband pulled a wallet out of the right pocket and a cell phone from the left.

"Drop them."

Both objects hit the floor.

"Come here."

Allen turned around but didn't move.

"Come here," Gabe repeated, but the husband remained frozen.

Gabe lowered the shotgun, stepped forward, and kicked Allen in the testicles. The man didn't even try to protect himself. Allen squeaked once and collapsed to the floor.

With the heel of his boot, Gabe stomped on the cell phone and sent bits of plastic about the room. He turned his attention to Sylvia. "What about you?"

"I don't have a phone." She wore a yellow sundress with no pockets.

"Grab the kid and go downstairs."

Sylvia stood and picked up the girl. The weight of the child in her arms barely slowed her.

"Get up," Gabe ordered Allen. The husband lay on the ground, moaning loudly and holding himself. "*Now.*"

Allen stood awkwardly and held the wall as he descended the staircase.

***

Sylvia and Taylor stood in the middle of the room. Their eyes were riveted to the sofa. Allen stopped when he saw what his wife and daughter were staring at.

On the couch was the cop. The top of his head was missing.

"What happened?" Gabe asked.

"He woke up." Harv grabbed Allen. "Come here."

The man allowed himself to be pulled away from his family. Harv shoved the husband.

"On the ground."

The accountant slowly kneeled, but it wasn't fast enough. Harv grabbed the back of Allen's neck and pushed him toward the floor. "On your face," he ordered.

Sylvia screamed and reached for her husband.

"Don't move," Gabe said. "Please."

"*Please*?" Harv smirked.

Gabe shrugged.

"Gimme the bag."

Harv climbed onto Allen's back. Gabe slipped off the backpack and tossed it to his partner. Harv pulled a length of rope out and tied up the husband.

"What are you going to do?" Sylvia asked.

Gabe's eyes flicked toward her husband.

Tears rolled down her face before she buried it in the crook of her child's neck.

Harv finished securing the accountant's hands behind his back. He bound his legs together at the knees and ankles. The process disgusted Gabe. Not because of what

Harv did, but because Allen didn't even resist when a rag was shoved into his mouth. The guy never struggled once. Gabe's lip curled at the thought that sheep fight harder when they're about to be shorn.

When Harv finished, he pointed at Sylvia. Sweat beaded on his forehead. "You're next."

Sylvia shook her head and held on to her daughter.

Harv's face reddened further. "Now."

The wife remained still, her arm tightening around her daughter.

Harv stood and stomped over to her. He leaned into her face and glowered. She turned her head. "Fine," he said. "I'll save the best for last."

He grabbed Taylor by the arm and yanked her away from Sylvia. Both mother and child screamed. Sylvia reached for her daughter but stopped when Gabe raised his gun.

Harv shoved the girl to the floor.

"Easy," Gabe said.

"Mind your business."

Taylor cried the entire time Harv tied her up. During the process, he told her to shut up, or he'd give her something to cry about.

Several minutes later, when he finished, Harv stood and glanced around. "Where's the head?"

"There's one upstairs," Gabe said.

"Isn't there one down here?"

With tears glistening on her cheeks, Sylvia stared at her daughter.

Harv clapped his hands several times to get her attention. "Where's the head?"

Sylvia blinked. "Head?"

"Commode? Crapper? Where is it?"

She pointed at the kitchen.

"Tie her up." Harv left the room without another word.

Sylvia spun toward Gabe. "Please," she whispered. "Let us—"

"Stop." Her pleading wouldn't win points with him. "Get on the ground."

She lay on her stomach and willingly put her hands behind her. He grabbed another piece of rope from the backpack and secured her hands and feet.

Just as Gabe finished, Harv walked back into the room. He carried a chair from the kitchen.

Harv grinned and talked fast. His attitude had changed since going to the bathroom. "All right, big boy," he said to Allen, "let's start this party."

He dropped the chair, then lifted the husband into it. Afterward, he tugged the rag from the accountant's mouth.

"Here's how this is going to work. You tell us what you told the cops, and we'll leave."

"I didn't say anything," Allen said.

Harv slapped him. "If you don't tell us what we want to know, I'm going to hurt you. If that doesn't work—" He pointed to the wife. "I'll hurt her. And if that doesn't work—" Harv pointed to the kid. "You know what happens then, right?"

Allen shook his head, panic evident in his eyes. "I swear I didn't tell them anything."

Harv's fist slammed into Allen's cheek. The accountant grunted, and his head lolled. Harv grabbed the husband by the hair.

"That's a dead cop right there. He wasn't hangin' out with you guys for fun. What did you tell them?"

"It's not what you think."

Harv punched him in the right eye. The chair tipped backward, and Allen fell helplessly onto his back. His feet kicked up into the air.

The wife and daughter lay on their stomachs and screamed.

Harv yanked the chair out from underneath the accountant and threw it across the room. "What did you tell them?"

"Nothing."

Harv kicked Allen in the side. "What did you give them?" he hollered.

With his arms behind his back, Allen curled up in a fetal position. Harv kicked the husband's hands. Gabe heard a bone break, and the man screamed.

"Stop!" Allen cried. "Stop!"

Harv bent over. "You gonna tell me?"

Allen continued to cry.

Harv straightened and clapped his hands. "Enough. We're done. On to phase two." He collected the chair, set it upright, then lifted Allen back into the seat. He put his face directly in front of the accountant. "Time for your wife."

Allen glanced at Sylvia. "No!"

"Tell us," Gabe said, "and he won't hurt her."

"You'll kill us no matter what." Allen's words ran together from fear.

"No, he won't."

When Allen closed his eyes and shook his head, Harv moved toward the woman.

"Let me move the kid out of the room," Gabe said.

Harv glared at him. "What?"

"She doesn't need to see this."

"Pussy."

"She's a kid."

"Worry about your job."

Harv grabbed Sylvia and slid her to an open spot on the floor. He straddled her chest and shoved a rag into her mouth. Her eyes widened, and she screamed into the cloth. Harv slapped her hard across the face.

Allen stared at the floor. Gabe grabbed his hair and wrenched his head up. "Watch."

Harv looked back at Allen. "Talk, or this will get worse."

The accountant kept his mouth shut. Gabe yanked his head backward by his hair. "That's your wife."

Gabe pushed the man's head back into place, so he could see what was about to happen.

Harvey Mott punched the woman in the eye and bounced her head off the floor. She passed out after that. Harv looked back again at the accountant.

"*Talk*," Gabe said.

Not getting the reaction he wanted, Harv pulled a knife from his pocket and opened the blade.

Allen shrieked, "I didn't say anything!"

Harv shrugged. "Too little, too late."

The accountant wildly shook his head. "I didn't tell them anything. She did! She found out and told the cops."

Harv relaxed for a moment and considered the man's words. Eventually, he sighed and turned back to the woman. He grabbed her sundress and yanked it tight. Then he cut and ripped it until it was completely open. When she spilled out, he turned back to the husband.

"Please," Allen whispered.

"Tell us what we need to know," Gabe said.

"I didn't say anything. She did."

Harv rubbed a hand over the woman's body. It wasn't sensual, and it wasn't even like he had an interest in the woman. It was like he was petting a dog. The kid watched as Harvey violated her mother.

"Hey," Gabe said to the girl. "Keep your eyes on me."

Harvey glanced back to see him talking to the kid. He frowned, stood, and closed his knife.

Allen whispered. "Please."

Gabe slapped him. "Do you know what he's going to do now?"

Harv headed out of the room. "Be right back."

"Where are you going?" Gabe asked.

"Restroom."

"Again?"

Harv extended his middle finger behind his back.

The kid's eyes locked onto her mother. When Sylvia came around, she was slow to realize what had happened.

Gabe pushed Allen out of his chair and he fell to the floor. He grunted but didn't bother protesting. He continued to cry for himself.

"Kid," Gabe said as calmly as possible. "I'm gonna move you. Don't be scared, okay?"

Taylor squirmed away as he reached for her. He lifted her and moved her to the furthest corner of the room. She leaned against the wall. The end of the sofa blocked her view of her mother. The girl shook, and tears streaked her face.

Harv came back just as Gabe was positioning her. "The fuck you doing?"

"She doesn't need to see this."

"You're losing it."

"I'm not the one running to the bathroom every five minutes." Gabe rubbed a finger under his nose.

Harv mimicked the motion, trying to dust off powder that was no longer there. "Fuck you."

The woman opened her eyes wider as Harv stood over her. He dropped onto her chest, and she screamed. Even though Gabe couldn't watch, he lifted Allen back into his chair so the husband could.

Harv hit Sylvia several times until she passed out again.

"What did you tell the cops?" Gabe asked. Before the words left his mouth, he knew the husband wouldn't admit to anything. He simply stared at his wife. Her face was now a bloody mess.

Harv slapped the unconscious woman a couple of times, then stood up. "The broad can't take a punch."

Allen mumbled something.

"What was that?"

"Screw you," the accountant whispered.

"Screw me?" Harv jerked his gun from the back of his waistband and fired a round into the woman's chest.

Allen bounced up and down in the chair while he screamed.

Gabe looked at the kid, and she stared directly at him from around the corner of the couch.

Harv stepped over to Allen and bent to face him directly. "Wanna say that again?"

Allen bowed his head and sobbed.

"Gonna start talking now?"

Harvey lifted the accountant's face. The man closed his eyes and wept.

Letting the husband's head fall back to his chest, Harv stepped back. "Time for the kid, I guess."

Allen jerked his head up.

"That got your attention. What did you tell the cops?"

"She was the one," the husband said and motioned toward his wife. "Not me. Not me!"

Harv clucked his tongue. "Wrong answer." When he turned toward the kid, Gabe blocked his path. "The fuck is wrong with you?"

"She's a kid."

"Get a grip."

Harv moved toward the girl, but Gabe grabbed him. He whirled around and pushed Gabe, who stumbled backward, fell to the floor, and landed partially on the woman's body.

After tucking his gun into his waistband, Harv grabbed the kid and lifted her. "You're gonna hate this." He dropped the kid to the floor in front of the accountant and pulled out his knife.

Gabe scrambled up and jumped. When he hit Harv, the man let go of the knife, and it clattered away. They rolled around, throwing punches into each other with little effect. Harv pushed off Gabe and went for his gun.

Rolling to his side, Gabe yanked his pistol from the back of his pants and fired.

Harv grunted, doubled over, then collapsed. His legs spasmed twice. Gabe grabbed Taylor by the arm and jerked her away. He fired once more at Harvey, and the man stopped moving.

The three of them remained silent for several minutes.

"Thank you," Allen whispered.

Taylor's body trembled as Gabe turned her away from the body of her mother.

Gabe moved in front of Allen. "What did you tell them?"

The husband shook his head.

"Your daughter needs a father. Tell me what I need to know, and I'll say you escaped."

Allen sucked in a breath of air and studied Gabe's eyes. Finally, he spilled it all. Every ounce of truth poured out.

Gabriel Forsberg focused on the words. He nodded as the husband spoke and did his best to remember things. When Allen finished speaking, Gabe leaned down until he was at eye level with the man.

"That's *exactly* what you told the cops. You didn't leave anything out?"

He nodded. "Exactly."

Gabe picked up the girl and cradled her in his arms. As he walked through the kitchen, he picked up a set of car keys from the table. He carried her outside and unlocked the car parked in front of the house. He placed her in the passenger seat. She never opened her eyes the entire time.

He walked back into the house, picked up the shotgun, and returned to the accountant. "You let my partner beat your wife."

Allen stared at the shotgun.

"Then he killed her, and you still didn't say anything."

His mouth slowly opened as Gabe touched the shotgun to his chest.

"You didn't say anything when he went for your daughter."

Allen shook his head.

"You should have told the truth sooner. It would have stopped all of this from happening."

"It wouldn't have made any difference." He sounded like a whimpering little boy. "You would have still killed us."

"No," Gabe said. "Only you."

***

He went outside and collected the can of gas from the rear of the house. He poured some on Allen, Sylvia, the cop, and Harv.

Gabe then wiped down the shotgun and tossed it next to Harv. It was stolen, so he wasn't worried about anyone tracing it back to him.

He laid newspapers over each of the bodies, trying his best to provide fuel for the beast that would soon consume the room.

On the way out, he lit several matches and started the fire.

Gabe climbed into the Lexus and started it. He pushed Taylor onto the passenger floorboard. "Be quiet," he said and backed the car away from the house.

***

He drove to where he had left the Chevy. He unloaded the kid and tucked her onto the passenger floorboard of his car. He then untied her and threw the rope into the woods.

Gabe wiped down everything he touched on the Lexus. Then he threw the keys into the woods.

They drove back toward Metaline Falls without the radio on. Taylor watched him the entire time.

About a mile outside town, he pulled over. Gabe lifted the kid onto the passenger seat. She pressed her body into the side door.

"I'm not gonna hurt you." He pointed down the road. "Walk that way. When you get to a store, any store, go inside and tell them who you are. Tell them what happened. Do you understand?"

She blinked several times but never said a word. Gabe reached across her and opened her door.

The girl slid out of the car but continued to make eye contact. He was taking a big gamble that she could identify him, but it was a risk he could live with. He couldn't live with the alternative.

"Step back," he said.

She took one hesitant step back.

Gabe pressed the accelerator, and the car lurched forward. The passenger door slammed shut.

The girl grew smaller in the rearview mirror.

He thought about turning around and making a run for Canada, but he didn't have a passport with him. Besides, the border guards would remember a guy like him.

Instead, he headed toward Spokane.

The drive would give him plenty of time to rehearse a lie about how Harvey died.

Notes

My first attempt at writing crime fiction was a short story—just a couple of pages long. It wasn't any good, but it succeeded in doing one thing—it existed. Even if it would never see publication, that simple story proved I could write something.

After the first one, I was hooked. I became a junkie for words. I couldn't get enough. I soon created all sorts of characters in terrible scenarios. Many of those stories would never see the light of day and for good reason.

It's okay that some of those early works were bad. I was experimenting and trying out new things. I learned the cadence of sentences and discovered the rhythm of dialogue. Musicians do this all the time. They noodle with riffs. Some are great. Some are crap. As fans, we only hear the ones that make our hearts race and our souls fly. Hopefully, that's what writers do as well.

That doesn't mean a lousy riff can't teach us something.

I wrote a short story once I knew wasn't right when I finished. Even though I edited the hell out of it, I couldn't get it where it needed to be. Regardless, I kept it. There was something inside that story that I believed in. My problem was I couldn't properly execute the idea at that time. Now, I'm glad I couldn't. Nearly twenty years later, I rescued it—the idea, not the story—and wrote a full-length novel from it. That's how *The Value in Our Lies* (the fifth novel in the 509 Crime Stories) came about.

I hope you enjoyed the short stories included in this collection. More than that, I hope you loved one of them above all the others. I'm not arrogant enough to believe you dug them all. I have several favorite albums where there is a song I always skip. I mean, I love Mötley Crüe, but do I love every song they've done? No, but I always come back to their albums and listen to those I love and occasionally skip those I don't. Just like that, I hope you've found a story or two that you'll come back and reread.

With that, let me share some notes about the included tales.

One of my favorite short stories, "**Angel**," came from my time on the police department. A homicide victim had a woman tattooed on his lower back. When I asked the investigating detective why a man would get a tattoo like that, she said, "It's a prison tattoo. He was somebody's woman."

And like that, a story was born.

"Angel" was first published by the now-defunct e-zine, *Crime Scene Scotland*. The editors loved the story but were hesitant to post it due to the subject matter of male rape. When they finally agreed to share the tale, they gave their readers an advisory warning. While I'm glad they provided a spot for my work, I've always thought the notice was a bit hypocritical. Many crime stories have been built around male-female rape, but one between two men was deemed too much for most readers.

"**The Grievance**" and "**The Death of Wilbur Pennington**" appeared in the Dark City Books' anthology, *Spokane is Still Deader than Dead*. This was before I had any inkling of what the 509 Crime Stories could be.

"The Death of Wilbur Pennington" came to me while listening to classical music one evening. I'm usually a hard rock guy, but I'll occasionally go down a musical genre rabbit hole. (In fact, I'm listening to jazz while writing these notes.) While Mozart's "Eine Kleine Nachtmusik" played, I imagined a detective studying a homicide scene. It was unlike any other vision of a detective I had. The guy seemed like a stuffed shirt, and I wondered how he would act at a crime scene.

"Loyalty Lost" was initially published in Koboca Publishing's *The Ex-Factor*. I updated the story and moved it out of Spokane. I couldn't have the central department in my police procedural series littered with bad cops.

"Murder by the Roadside" has already been published as a standalone tale in the 509 universe. The story comes from a lyric in the Duran Duran song, "Wild Boys." I love when a story idea comes from hearing a familiar song.

Yes, I know I've now admitted to listening to classical, jazz, and '80s pop while claiming to be a metal guy. I'm well-rounded. What can I say?

So, I was listening to "Wild Boys," and the lyric in question came on. I immediately imagined a county sheriff standing roadside, investigating a murder. I had so much fun writing Sheriff Tom Jessup that he appeared again in *The Blind Trust*, the third novel in the 509 Crime Stories.

Several stories in this collection are getting their initial publication. "Lot Lizards," "Inheritance of the Meek," "A Lonely Place of Suffering," "The Accident," "A Brother's Burden," and "Whisper" are being exposed to readers for the first time.

I hate serial killers. I shouldn't have to say that, but there are way too many movies, TV shows, and books glorifying these guys. I mean, if the world had as many serial killers as some writers love to focus on, the world would be a dead place. I mean that literally.

However, I broke down and wrote about one in "**Lot Lizards**." I didn't want to do the trendy thing and write about a serial killer that kills only bad people. *Dexter* has that entire angle covered. I also didn't want to write about a serial killer that murdered in a super-complicated fashion. So many have done that I wouldn't know where to start. So, I asked, "What's a serial killer's vacation look like?" If you've already read it, you know it's not for the faint of heart.

"**Inheritance of the Meek**" was another short story I wrote wherein I loved the idea, but I didn't like how it initially worked. I put it away and let it simmer for fifteen years. Then, as the world of the 509 grew, I pulled the story back out and finally realized what the problem was. I had written the piece in the first-person point-of-view when it wanted to be in third person. Once I changed that, everything clicked, and I now dig the story.

"**A Lonely Place of Suffering**" featured one of my favorite short story characters—alcoholic, former police officer Ronald Brenner. He was a sad guy, shuffling his way through life until his neighbor was murdered. Then he found a reason to care about something again. I hope he shows up in a future story.

"**Whisper**" gave some backstory on Tiger, the violent pimp who first appeared in *The Mean Street*. The story also took place in the Hope Apartments, which has its own anthology (*The Eviction of Hope*).

I appreciate you sticking to the end and reading through these notes. These short stories have a fond place in my heart, which is probably weird since they're tales of murder.

Hopefully, you've enjoyed a couple of them enough to come back and reread them another day. Skip the ones you don't like. As I mentioned before, I love Mötley Crüe, but I've always skipped song five on *Shout at the Devil* for the past thirty-five years. But I still enjoy the album and would recommend it to any lover of hard rock.

Colin
Spokane, Washington
Summer 2021

About the Author

Colin Conway is the creator of the 509 Crime Stories, a series of novels set in Eastern Washington with revolving lead characters. They are standalone tales and can be read in any order.

He also created the Cozy Up series which pushes the envelope of the cozy genre. Libby Klein, author of the Poppy McAllister series, says *Cozy Up to Death* is "Not your grandma's cozy."

Colin co-authored the Charlie-316 series. The first novel in the series, *Charlie-316*, is a political/crime thriller that has been described as "riveting and compulsively readable," "the real deal," and "the ultimate ride-along."

He served in the U.S. Army and later was an officer of the Spokane Police Department. He has owned a laundromat, invested in a bar, and run a karate school. Besides writing crime fiction, he is a commercial real estate broker.

Colin lives with his beautiful girlfriend, three wonderful children, and a codependent Vizsla that rules their world.

Find out more at colinconway.com